DOG DAZE OF SUMMER

The Dog Tail Detective Series

MARYANNE VANDYKE

ISBN-13: 978-0-578-54080-1

Dedication

In memory of Dick Armstrong who first treated his granddaughters, Jessica and Hillary, to the stories of Sam, the super dog. Years later, Dick and I purchased our puppy, Sam. Soon after, when Dick realized he was not strong enough to provide Sam his daily walks, Sam moved to my house and we began our life journey. Thank you, Dick, for providing love and laughter to my life. May these stories be a tribute to your giving nature and love of our boy, Sam.

Acknowledgments

I'd like to thank the many people who helped make this book possible through their generosity by providing advice and encouragement. Without all of you, Sam would never have shared his memoir.

Laura Logsdon Buchanan, my darling daughter, who used her organizational skills to critique and inspire me along the path to my story's end.

Pamela Foster, author of Noisy Creek, who as developmental editor guided Sam's story and became my mentor and dear friend.

Leona and Jack Applegate who Sammy knows as his "other" parents, for their care and love of the boy dog and his story.

Billie and Lizabeth Anne Johnson who good-naturedly allowed me to read Dog Daze to them, reminding me when Izzie forgot her pink overnight bag.

Eowana Peters Krieg who reminded me women in southern novels are crazy because of the heat.

Judy Duncan, Owner Bella Vista Funeral Home and Crematory, who provided invaluable information for the death scenes.

Teachers: Alison Taylor-Brown, Jayne Stewart, Jeannine Lauer and Gene King who reminded me to show not tell.

The ladies of Newcomers of Rutherford County, Tennessee and Senior Center of Smyrna, Tennessee who encouraged and supported Sam's journey.

The staff at AIW Press, who bound years of work into a neat red package.

Prologue

The little girl's giggles could be heard down the long dark hallway.

Six-year old Izzie sat cross-legged, hidden in her customary play spot behind the black leather sofa in her daddy's library. She tied the bow under the puppy's chin and adjusted the bonnet around the floppy ears of Stella, her new Shih Tzu puppy. A hand-carved wooden kaleidoscope and a dolly in a red taffeta dress rested on the rug beside her. They were all hidden in the child's customary play spot.

The child hummed a tune while adjusting the dolly's red dress, then picked up the kaleidoscope from the rug. The puppy watched and listened with its head cocked.

Daddy Matt, knowing she was hiding there, leaned forward in his wheelchair. He was spinning another exciting yarn, this time about how, years ago, he shot the huge elk whose head now hung above his desk on the walnut paneled wall.

The smile on his sun-weathered face told her of the happiness he felt in the moment. He spun his wheelchair around, recalling the crisp autumn day when years ago he'd made the incredible shot.

He remembered spying the animal through the forest of fall colors. He remembered the crunch of dried leaves under his boots. Slowly he had lifted the gun to his eye and taken aim. Bright sunlight flashed through the trees onto the elk's horns.

The sun now flashed through the library window onto the mounted elk's horns. The sun also flashed through the window onto the little girl's kaleidoscope. Matt related how he lifted his gun higher and higher. Izzie, picked up the kaleidoscope, put it to her eye and spun the sphere faster and faster.

Explosion! A shot. One, no, two.

The elk fell. No, no, it was Daddy who fell. His body slowly slid from his wheelchair. Glass tumbled, a kaleidoscope of color splattered, the rug buried under sparkling glass and blood.

Alligator boots dashed across the worn Persian rug. Light reflected from a belt buckle. Izzie's heart pounded. Who else was there? Daddy on the carpet. Colors fuzzy. Red, too much red. Red blood covering the front of her daddy's body. Daddy's red shirt. Dolly's red dress.

A hefty black woman screamed as she rubbed her hands on an apron covered in beet juice and bacon drippings. "Jesus, Mary, Joseph. God, help dis po' child."

Falling, falling, falling. Colors blurred. Izzie fell into a dark hole—absent of all color.

Izzie slept the sleep of a child taking an unguided, frightening step toward becoming an adult.

Chapter 1

Twenty Years Later

July 4, eight-thirty in the morning

"Get a move on, Izzie, your Love Sponge has to piddle," I woofed in my nicest whine while wagging my tail in my special loving manner. My paws covered my ears to block the first notes of "How Much is that Doggie in the Window?" The song from the cell phone rang, again, and again, and again.

I yawned and did my downward dog and a couple forward stretches. The humidity caused my bones to ache. Sweat on my paws told me it was going to be another hot, muggy July day. We, in Memphis, Tennessee call these the dog days of summer.

I should introduce myself. My name is Sam. I am a Shih Tzu. My life is simple, and my wants are few. But, right then, I needed to piddle. Just a normal function. I don't understand why people make such a ta-do about it. On that hot summer day my need to piddle had a higher priority than being offered a thick raw juicy T-bone.

Shih Tzu's can easily wait five to six hours. Back in the day, long before time grayed my muzzle and took its toll on my bladder, when Izzie, my Sweetie, was out late and forgot to put me outside, I could go even longer. Give me a nice bush, not too far from the front door, and I could lift my leg for a full minute. However, even in my glory days, this wait got me really out-of-sorts. I was getting that grumpy feeling then.

"Izzie, please get out of bed, answer that phone and take me out to some grass," I growled.

At that point, I'd have welcomed some old dried leaves. Although, old dried leaves are something we didn't have in Memphis, at least not in the high rent district.

I lived with Izzie, my darling Momma, my Sweetie, in this home called a loft. It was an old four-story warehouse that Matt, Izzie's father, bought years before he died. He turned the whole building into lofts which he rented for something called big bucks. Izzie said we were all cohabitating. We didn't actually live together but everyone used the same yard. She called it a courtyard although I never saw any lawyer-people holding court.

My Izzie stretched. She covered her ears. Man, I had a real big problem that morning. She pulled the pillow over her head. With one hand she grabbed for the phone on the bedside table. It fell to the floor.

"Damn," she groaned as her long-tapered fingers strained to reach under the bed. She had been up way too late. I need to mention, she was a bit of a klutz.

Throwing a pillow off the bed, Izzie sat up, listened to what was being said, and began to tremble.

"No, no, you're wrong. Are you sure? I talked to her last night."

Holding the phone in one hand, Izzie grabbed me with her Love-Sponge-Hug and sobbed. I squirmed to get loose from her tight grasp, then thought better of it when I heard the voice on the phone. It was Jake, telling us to come home to Nesbit as soon as we could.

"Patrick just called to say his grandmother Clarabelle was found dead early this morning by his granddad, Guffin. His grandad had returned home around five o'clock in the morning, returning from a cattle delivery in Jackson, Tennessee for our grandfather. He found Clarabelle in her La-Z-Boy. At first, he thought she was asleep but then he touched her, and her arm fell to her side. She was cold and wasn't breathing. He immediately called Dr. Daut."

"Couldn't the doctor revive her?" Izzie grabbed the edge of the sheet and dabbed her eyes.

"He didn't try. It was obvious she had been dead a few hours. They brought the ambulance and the coroner pronounced her dead at the scene."

We Shih Tzu's are a pretty tough breed but I'm telling you my long eye lashes were getting wet. I gave Izzie my big-eyed look and cocked my head sideways to hear more.

"Was it her heart?"

"Probably, she may have been sleeping and just passed on. They found a spilled Coke and her bed pillow on the floor."

I heard Jake tell Izzie Patrick thought he could leave Nashville within the hour, as soon as he got in contact with two professors. He should be in Nesbit, Mississippi by early afternoon.

I'd better take a moment to explain to you. Jake is the half-brother to Izzie and her older sister Hannah. It was their father who was murdered when Izzie was a little girl. Jake was five when Matt married their mother, Olivia. Hannah was born seven months later. Patrick is Clarabelle's grandson.

"I can't believe you're telling me this," Izzie sobbed. "Clarabelle called around eleven last night. I was just getting in from a gal-party on the boat. She said she wanted me to know her heart problem had worsened, and she could go to The Lord at any time. She said she had talked about a lot of things to Father Sims last week in her Saturday confession.

"We were still talking when Clarabelle heard a truck coming toward her house. I am sure she said the truck looked like the old blue Dodge Father Sims drives, but it couldn't have been him at that time of night."

I tucked my head under Izzie's pillow and whined. She stroked my gray and black fur as if I were the one who needed comforting

"Probably not him. I'll shower and get there soon," Izzie said.

"I'll call Hannah and your mother to let them know you're on your way," Jake replied.

If she didn't take me to piddle soon a lot more would be wet than her in the shower. It had been an alarming, long night and the day was not starting off any better.

I lingered at the bathroom door. The hot steam from Izzie's shower filled the air. The sweet smell of Jasmine coupled with the steam helped my black nose breath better. Izzie quickly showered and flung on a crisp white shirt tied at the waist over skinny jeans and leather Adidas flip flops. She stuffed some clothes in a little pink bag, threw her purse over her shoulder, grabbed my sack of dog food and leash and we headed to elevator.

I loved this little gliding room. My tummy went bump, bump as it took us down four floors, then I darted through the front door. Just as a blast of hot air hit my wet nose, I found my favorite bush. Ahhhh, relief.

Chapter 2

I lived a perfect dog life in the loft because I had lots of canine friends. I was, and still am, a social kind of guy. The Doberman, Sabbath, sometimes left good meat bones in the courtyard and I knew all his hiding places. He was one hundred pounds of muscle with a gentle side few knew but me. Little Daisy sprinted toward me whenever I went to the courtyard. I could tell she had a crush on me. She was also a Shih Tzu and a good looker. Little Daisy called me, Sammy, the Stud. Her black and white curly locks sometimes enticed me but, enough of that. Izzie took care of my pleasure bone a few years back when I was a little guy.

Izzie hooked my leash on my halter, and we hurried toward the underground parking garage. I hustled my short legs to keep up. We were soon on our way to Nesbit, a thirty-minute drive on I-55 south from Memphis. We rode most of the trip in complete silence.

My favorite place was riding above the back seat watching through the window to see where we'd been. You should understand that rear windows don't go up and down like the side ones. My sweet Izzie was stern with me if I stuck more than my nose out to get some smells. By the time we crossed the line from Tennessee into Mississippi, Izzie was rubbing the nape of her neck. I think Izzie was in her dark place again. She hadn't even picked up my gift I left back there on the grass in the courtyard.

Sometimes I had trouble understanding Izzie when she half muttered, half talked. She did this when she was edgy and in her dark place. I gave my sweet momma some slack and paid attention as best I could by staring at the back of her head.

"Clarabelle had been closer to me than my own mother. Although I'm sure Mother Olivia loved me, she just wasn't very motherly. Clarabelle had been like a Mother to us three children and my little dog."

The dog was, of course, my Grandog, Stella. The three children were Clarabelle's grandson, Patrick, a handsome young man, his dark brown skin was nearly as appealing as his smart quips. Hannah, Izzie's older sister, a striking blond with the deep blue eyes of her mother. My Izzie, tanned and toned with hazel eyes of her daddy, was the youngest of the children.

Hannah and Izzie had been the little girls in Clarabelle's life. Clarabelle was the one who came upon the death scene of Mr. Matt and carried little Izzie out of the room. It was she, not Olivia, who sat with the child day after day until she awoke from her coma.

My sweet momma was, still is, the only purpose for my existence. I'm pleased to say I am her constant companion. In my puppy years, I learned her moods and inclinations. Growing older, I realized when I shared Izzie's hurts and joys I felt as they were my own. I knew Momma almost as much as she knew herself. Her soul is part of my soul.

I remember the first days Izzie and I moved into the warehouse. Clarabelle came up to Memphis to help us get settled. Izzie's mother, Olivia, never did any work that I ever saw. Each morning Izzie would leave us to open boxes while she went to work at St. Jude's. She worked something called PRN which I'd heard Izzie say meant she can work whenever she wants, even if it is only a couple days a week.

From the loft, Izzie could walk to the hospital or to the Memphis marina on Mud Island. That's where she kept a really big cruiser. That boat was so long my short little legs cried stop by the time I ran from one end to another. I thought it was called the bow to stern, but I could have been mistaken.

After a day of unpacking boxes to fill the closets and shelves, Clarabelle and I walked to the cruiser and Izzie would meet us there for one of Clarabelle's tasty meat pies. Juicy gravy was around all the meat and carrot pieces. I would get a nice serving 'cause I'm such a good boy—so said Clarabelle.

I had my special puppy box in the officer's head. This was boat talk for bathroom. It was fun to watch Izzie clean my puppy box. At least I didn't smell like that cat she had for a while. I growled at the poor thing until it said bye-bye and left. I really didn't dislike cats, but this one was always purring and rubbing on me. A stud dog like me sure didn't want to smell like a cat. I think Clarabelle took it home with her to the farm.

The cruiser was also part of Izzie and Hannah's inheritance from their daddy, Matt. It was new back in the eighties and was still a fine ship twenty years later. One-time Izzie, Hannah, and I cruised down the Mississippi all the way to the Gulf. I was so brave I jumped into the cold water and lived to tell about it. Momma hummed a tune as she dried me with her big red-checked beach towel. She hummed a lot when she was happy.

I was very brave because Momma always puts me into my bright yellow safety vest the minute we get on the boat. My momma called me her "Love Sponge" and told everyone how much I loved the water.

She was very cautious, perhaps because she was a nurse who has seen a lot of boat accidents in the ER.

I still enjoy a good swim, but back in my youth I was an excellent swimmer. Taught by the best—my Izzie. She won lots of awards for diving and swimming in her teen years. All her shiny golden trophies were behind a glass case in the salon in the middle of the ship.

People down here in Memphis said Miss Izzie was a great long-distance swimmer. We don't ever tell our age in the South. She was only twenty-six, but folks still called her Miss Izzie.

Important responsibilities were part of my job as Izzie's constant companion. I had to be on constant alert to watch out for my sweet momma. She was graceful in the water, but a real train wreck on dry land. She could trip over her own feet. My toys were another matter. She even tripped over my green fuzzy turtle she brought me from Tahiti. Beats me how this happened. My conclusion was she was always in a hurry and never looked down, except to pat me, of course.

Anyway, this Miss business, I think is a Southern thing. Sometimes I called her Sweet Momma and she answered calling me her Love Sponge. I lovingly nudged her, then gave a glance from under my long black lashes. I knew this look was good for at least two treats.

Most members of the Memphis Yacht Club love dogs and just adored me. They were the ones who introduced me to raw steak and asparagus. I still love steak and asparagus.

Now, don't get me wrong. I've never been a snob, but I did know a bit about the better things in human and doggie life. Sometimes we "pinch our pennies" like Clarabelle said Mr. Matt used to do. Clarabelle had the nicest way of speaking. She told me Mr. Matt would come in her kitchen and make sho' all de' scraps of bread were saved to make bread puddin'. Funny though, he didn't even like bread puddin'. So much for pinching those pennies.

All the dogs in the family liked Clarabelle, but I don't think y'all would've known her as we canines did. She was the nanny who came from Memphis to care for little Izzie and her older sister, Hannah. The girls grew up down in Nesbit, Mississippi, about thirty minutes south of Memphis. Clarabelle and her husband, Mac, lived on the farm and worked for the girl's parents.

My Grandog, Stella, stood close to Izzie, then hid under the sofa on the day Izzie's daddy was shot. Grandog told Mommadog that Clarabelle began screaming and waving her hands, shouting "Jesus, Mary, Joseph, Jesus, Mary, Joseph. God help us all."

Little Izzie had slumped to the floor and Clarabelle assumed she had been shot too. Izzie had fainted, but hysterical Clarabelle could not revive her and believed her dead. Someone yelled to get that baby to the hospital.

Izzie was in a coma for three months.

Grandog Stella, a puppy at that time, was shaking in fear with all the confusion. Later she would be called the Little Lion, but at that time she scurried behind the black sofa to hide. They had been playing there when the tall man in the buckskin jacket slid behind the door of the study. Puppy Stella saw him, then heard a deafening sound and people came running into the room. Until the day she died, Grandog Stella hated and feared the buckskin man with his fine polished boots and shiny belt buckle.

Clarabelle was a great one to tell secrets to us dogs. Puppy Stella's fears developed because every day Izzie was in the coma, Clarabelle took puppy Stella with her to the hospital, and sneaked her in under a towel in the basket of food for the day. The day Izzie woke, sure enough, there was Stella sitting beside her waiting to give her kisses.

Being a good judge of character was in my genes from Grandog Stella. She was nearly blind in her old age, but her brain was sharp. While I nursed from my Mommadog she growled telling me the smells to remember when we met a bad person. All my family of Shih Tzus loved Clarabelle. She was older when Izzie and I would visit the family, but she always made time from her chores to walk me. She talked as we watched the robins pull worms from the damp, soggy Mississippi soil. Clarabelle liked to talk to me, probably because I never talked back.

Nevertheless, I did pick up on every word she said. I'm not a snitch but you would be surprised to learn some of the secrets Clarabelle shared with me on those long walks. She had heard the story about how my Izzie was conceived and even more about the relationship between Father Sim's and Uncle Jessie. Then to top it all off, she knew things about the day Matt died. Things she said she knew but no one ever asked her about. She told me her ironing board was her safety net, whatever that meant.

Then Clarabelle died. And everything changed.

I feared we were driving toward a sad situation. A situation which reminded my momma of another loss, the loss of her daddy Matt. Her experience that terrible day was always a dark place in her memories, a place she went sometimes as she held me tight. She often scared me in her sleep when she sobbed and thrashed about. Then she lost Clarabelle. Izzie found it difficult to function without those weekly phone calls from someone she'd loved so much.

I believed there was more to her death than we knew. We Shih Tzu's are good thinkers and smellers, so I've got a great nose for these things. I needed to do some sniffing around when we got to Nesbit.

On the outskirts of town, Izzie finally broke her silence.

"Sammy, don't you know Mother will be flustered and in a dither about her annual Dog Daze of Summer party? It's really a Fourth of July Barbeque but now she'll say it's being ruined because of Clarabelle's death. Mother makes herself the center of the universe and can always find someone to blame things on, even if they are dead.

I wagged my tail and gave her a knowing look. I choose not to answer 'cause Izzie didn't dogspeak. No problem. I've read her thoughts all my life. That was not one of her better moments, so best to stare ahead and not bark.

"The party is scheduled to start at five o'clock this evening. Now with Clarabelle's death, Mother will not be so confident things will run smoothly. She always left Clarabelle to check on the caterers. I suppose she will need me and Hannah to check on all the final arrangements for her."

Lost in our thoughts, we were silent the rest of the drive.

Chapter 3

Normally when we went to Nesbit, we drove straight to Mother Olivia's house, but not that day. We made a sharp right and headed towards Jake's.

Mommadog told me Jake was only five when Matt married Olivia. Matt had been divorced for several years from Jake's mother, Janice, his high school sweetheart. Shortly after he started dating Olivia she learned she was pregnant. Olivia was eighteen and preferred to raise her baby, Hannah, as a single mother but that was frowned upon in the eighties. Matt pleaded with her, he wanted to do right and marry. Olivia's parents, who had a cattle and construction business with Matt, saw him as the perfect husband for their daughter despite their ten-year age difference.

Dust blew up around the car as Izzie took the road to the Lodge, as Jake called his home. It was also Izzie's retreat. She had a special connection there. Jake had incorporated many of her ideas when she was in high school and college as he remodeled the one-hundred-year-old cabin to become a rustic showplace. Years earlier the back side of the lodge had served as the servant's quarters. At that time the old hand-hewn beams were a very masculine setting for Jake's renowned Navaho rug and art collection.

We turned off the dirt road. Under a veil of old Magnolia trees, we followed the drive leading to Jake's home. Majestic trees, their aged bark, black as night, lined the grey gravel drive leading to a circle driveway. The azaleas, absent of their radiant spring red color, lined the circle leading to the front porch. Mommadog told me that Grandog, Stella, even in her later years, would bark at the abundance of squirrels that ran the porch railing of weathered hand-hewn logs.

The circle drive veered to the left leading to the newest addition, a three-car garage completed that past spring. From the garage a breezeway led to the back veranda and the kitchen's screened door. The lap pool and cabana with its outdoor kitchen, which would've made Julia Child squeal with delight, lie just beyond.

Please understand, I had never met this Julia lady, but Izzie talked about her sometimes when we were in the kitchen, so she must have been a cooking friend of Izzie's. Just the week before Izzie said to me "I drank the same wine as Julia. Do you think I'll cook better now?"

How would I know, I never drank the stuff? Sometimes her questions weren't worth my time to answer.

Though the red azaleas had faded in that sultry heat of July, stark white rhododendrons surrounding the area were in full bloom. I felt my black nose twitch with excitement and barked my happy bark, so everyone knew we were there. I loved the good whiffs in Jake's yard and especially seeing my very best dog-friend, Buddy, Jake's chocolate Lab.

Izzie unhooked my leash. I jumped from the car and got a whiff of the rhododendrons. How I loved the country smells. After leaving my mark on several bushes for my pal, I trotted behind Izzie toward the lodge.

"There you are on the veranda." Izzie ran toward Jake. "I'm so glad you're home. Can you believe, we've lost our sweet Clarabelle? How could such a good heart be so weak? Do you believe she had a heart attack?"

Jake laid aside a book, rose from the lounge chair, and hurried toward us. He took Izzie in his arms, gently pushed her hair out of her eyes and gave her a comforting hug. I fidgeted next to him but barely got a pat on my head. That was okay 'cause Izzie needed more comforting than I did.

"We are going to have to wait for the medical examiner's report to be sure," he said with a muffled sigh. "You know your mother's waiting for you? Your sister, Hannah, is already there."

"Yes, I'm sure she is. I just couldn't face Mother's babble first thing. I do understand why she wants to go ahead with her annual Dog Daze party. We'd have to call too many people if we canceled," she said. "I talked to her before I left Memphis and she's more concerned about her party than what happened to Clarabelle. So, let her have her damned party. I am totally disinterested in her annual barbeque and honestly—I just don't care."

Jake opened the screened door for us. I gave the bushes a final sniff and trotted behind.

Normally I rolled around on Jake's Indian rugs and got scolded, but that day I thought better of the whole thing and decided to go find my big pal. He was sound asleep on the sun porch, so I curled up beside him and pretended to get some shut eye. Even Buddy's slow rhythmic snore did not help my mood. My Sweetie had me worried, so I cocked my ears and listened to the sounds coming from the kitchen.

"How can you look so ravishing on a hot day like this?" Jake gave Izzie another hug.

"Tight jeans, a white shirt and good makeup is all it takes to get a compliment from you." She smiled a Mona Lisa kind of smile.

"Sure. Especially the jean part," he teased.

I wasn't sure what a Mona Lisa smile looked like, but Jake said it a lot when he talked to Izzie. The glass of red liquid he handed her dripped water from the humidity in the air.

"Thanks, this tastes like your special cucumber Bloody Mary."

"Sure is, made just the way y'all like it."

"Have you talked to Guffin or Patrick?" she asked.

Mac Guffin was Clarabelle's husband and Patrick was their only grandchild. He came to live with them when he was three after his mother and dad separated, his mother leaving to work in Chicago. He was a playmate to Izzie and Hannah and a serious student. Like many young black men of his day, Patrick overcame his financial struggles. He earned a medical degree and became a professor in the Medical School at Meharry Medical College in Nashville, Tennessee. Guffin, like Clarabelle, worked for the Bradford family, Izzie's parents.

"Yes, Patrick called to say they would be meeting Father Sims and the funeral director to make arrangements. He wondered if you, Hannah, and I would come over tomorrow and go through the house. He wants to minimize items of Clarabelle's, so his grandad won't be reminded of her everywhere. He knew y'all would be busy today with your mother's barbeque."

"Tomorrow will work. Now, just give me a few minutes to gather my thoughts, finish this drink, and I'll be off. I'm sure Mother and Hannah are busy by now amending plans with the caterer. There will be fireworks and I guess Uncle Jessie will sing. Mother always likes having him around. Her friends seem to like his rugged looks and the expensive western clothes he wears. He showers her with attention and compliments. She always says, 'He's your Daddy's brother and the only member of the family worth speaking to.'"

"Yeah, times have sure changed," Jake said. "When our Dad married Olivia, I was just a little boy, but I remember how she called Jessie white trash because he ran the cockfights after his dad was killed. Then he made it big in Nashville after singing and playing Memphis Blues on Stax records. Now he's down here a lot and sings for every holiday party. But, remember he is your only uncle and he sure can sing a good tune."

"I could use a good song right now. One of his melancholy, soul searching songs would accurately fit my mood. Guess I'd better find Sammy and drive on to mother's house. Here boy, where are you? Oh look, Jake, they're sound asleep and even snoring together. Two happy guys. Wake up Sammy. It's time to go."

I scratched an itch in that hard-to-reach spot behind my ear. My dear Sweetie, you'd think by now you would know when I'm faking it.

"Right, sleeping is what we should be doing."

"Oh, Jake, are you sure you're my big brother?"

"Just kidding. You know I'm always here for you, right? If the pool needs any attention, let me know. Buddy and I'll be there about four o'clock. Call if y'all need me to help sooner."

Buddy and I had enjoyed a great rest. Maybe I did doze off for a few minutes. I seem to remember a happy dream about burying a T-bone among Olivia's prize-winning hibiscus.

Chapter 4

My nose twitched every time I caught a whiff of meat. Maybe steak. Maybe ribs. I hurried toward the smell as fast as my short legs would move. Olivia's guests, some I recognized as her Mah Jongg ladies, blocked my way but not to worry. I ran between them as they handed their car keys to the parking guys. Izzie called the parking guys, valets. An odd word. They looked like regular guys to me. Several guests approached the area ahead of us.

We were all greeted by the mouthwatering aroma of hickory smoke, tomatoes, cumin and those secret ingredients of Big Al's Supreme Barbeque Sauce. His famous chicken and ribs tempted even the non-hungries to sample the meat that Izzie said would fall off the bone. Saved me a lot of gnawing.

We stood in line visiting with neighbors, ready to get our plate of goodies, when Izzie spied Father Sims through the crowd. She ran to catch up with him. I reluctantly left the allure of meat behind and dashed after her.

"There you are, Father. So glad you could come." Izzie gathered her hair back and retied her ponytail. "Such a scorching day is even more unbearable because of Clarabelle's death. Isn't it difficult for us to feel happy on such a tragic day? How all our lives have changed for the worse."

"My child, we all loved Clarabelle, but God has his plans for her now. You know she was having a lot of discomfort with her heart condition. She is at rest now with Him." Father bent down and gave my long ears a loving tug and began to cough.

A small tidbit came out of his pocket along with a packet of cigarettes. Oh, I really did want to like this priest, but every time I was around him my nose started to burn. It's probably those terrible Pall Malls. When we had been there for the family Easter dinner Izzie told Jake something life-threatening was wrong with the priest's lungs. My nose told me something grim was about to happen.

"I miss her already," Izzie sobbed. "What about poor Guffin? He has that bad leg and no one to care for him. And dear Patrick, just beginning his professorship at Meharry Medical College. It will be difficult to leave his grandad here in Nesbit for his teaching assignments. He will be spending a lot of time on the road between here and Nashville. Perhaps he can get a position in Memphis, perhaps St. Jude's. He would be a lot closer."

Father Sims scratched my right ear. He knew what I liked. The perspiration on his forehead told me he was hot, like me.

"Now, now, Izzie, these problems are in the Lord's hands. He's given us a beautiful sunny day, though I admit it is very humid. You should enjoy your mother's lovely party. Put your concerns in the hands of the Lord."

He lit a cigarette, turned and slowly walked toward the crowd. Smoke rose heavenward as he disappeared into the throng. The priest seemed older. His limp more pronounced than when I sat at his feet under the Easter table and he slipped me tiny tidbits of Virginia ham.

Earlier that day when Izzie and I arrived, the band members were putting the finishing touches on the bandstand. What a mess. They uncovered my stash of old bones. Good musicians, but sloppy carpenters. Hammers, nails, and extra lumber scattered in various piles behind the stage made it tough for Buddy and me to find all our bones. We dug over by the flagpole and found two that could be good if the tidbit treats were few.

The stage looked great. Twinkling café lights and orange lanterns strung above the small bandstand swayed as music drifted toward the pool. Father Sims approached the area and got a nod from Jessie who was on stage singing the decade old hit by Merle Haggard, "That's the Way Love Goes".

Father sluggishly walked to a picnic table beside the band stand and I trotted right behind him. He was known to be good for a few bites of meat if I played my cards right. As he started to eat, I put my paws together and bowed my head. 'Bless us, oh Lord, for these gifts which we are about to receive.'

I looked like I was saying my mealtime prayer. Tap. Tap. Tap. My plumed tail smacked the grassy lawn expressing joy for what was about to come. I heard Father Sims emit a hearty chuckle. He bought it! Several bites of chicken followed. It may have been a humid summer day, but those dog days could also be great treat days for dogs like me who knew how to make good friends happy.

I was attacking a tasty morsel when Olivia stopped to say hello and began to chat with the priest. I had a good spot under the picnic table to hear their conversation. Buddy found me and slipped under the table ever so quietly. I shared some of Father's chicken scraps as we chewed and listened.

"I declare, Jessie is playing some great melodies tonight." Olivia swept her bangs from her face. A tall, willowy blonde in her early fifties, still polished and gracious, still the Southern beauty. A few deep frown lines from too many night-caps were beginning to show on her porcelain skin. As always, she avoided me. She looked directly at the priest.

Olivia tapped her foot to Jessie's music. "You and Jessie have been friends since you were sent to Saint Anne's directly out of seminary, right?"

"Yes, as a very young priest I was sent to a Southern Missouri cotton farming area to serve the tenant farmers as well as the prosperous of Caruthersville. It was there in that rural community I met your husband, Matt, God rest his soul, and Jessie. Matt was a teenager, three years older than Jessie, and seven years younger than me. Matt was a fine young man, but he lacked the God-given tenor voice of Jessie. Jessie sang in the church choir which I directed."

"Yours has been a close friendship, hasn't it?" Olivia asked.

My ears perked. Olivia's voice dripped with resentment. I could smell the bitterness coming from her pores.

"Yes, Jessie and I, although from different backgrounds, became friends immediately. As a young priest I was fascinated by the local people and activity surrounding the cockfights that Jessie and his Father ran on the sly."

Father scratched my right ear, my good listening ear.

"The farmers with a week's pay in hand, bankers and store owners with cash in their pockets, as well as gamblers from Memphis looked upon those Friday night gatherings as their secret society. The abundance of beer and moonshine allowed for an evening of fun without their women folk asking questions. My time in the confessional was a busy one."

The priest dabbed the perspiration from his forehead with a monogramed linen handkerchief. "But that was a long time ago. So much has happened since then. You may not know that within six months of arriving there, my first parish, my vow of poverty became threatened due to the death of both my parents in a car wreck.

My tummy was full of the tidbits the good priest had provided. I came out from under the picnic table to better position myself for a good ear scratch. A sad expression covered the priest's normally pleasant face as he removed his hand from my head and stared into the distance. Perhaps he was remembering something, something too dreadful to remember.

"But Father, I declare, I've heard you did wonderful things with your inheritance. When you were assigned to our parish here in Nesbit, we heard about the wonderful things you had done. You remodeled the rectory, built a parish hall and repaired Saint Anne's Church of Caruthersville to become a small jewel settled at the edge of a cotton field."

Clarabelle always said he did a lot for his parishioners. Last summer, over a year ago, Izzie and I came to visit Olivia on Mother's Day. Clarabelle, Izzie, and Olivia were visiting on Olivia's front porch. No, not me. I had seen that black and white fuzzy barn cat lurking behind those big green pots of red geraniums. I ran over to go show him who was boss of the yard, but it didn't turn out so good for me. That pussy had a real nasty temper and he smelled really bad.

I skulked back to the porch in time to hear Clarabelle say the parishioners only whispered about his close friendship with Jessie and his weakness for betting on the cockfights. Sometimes they looked suspiciously at each other and questioned among themselves when he drove to the fights in his new blue Dodge Ram, wearing old jeans and a workman's shirt.

I rested at Clarabelle's feet and cleaned the smell of that nasty barn cat from my paws. "He forgave them their sins," she said, "and they forgave him his addictions."

I had to think about her statement over a cool bowl of water.

Chapter 5

I lapped a cool drink and panted less as the humidity of the evening gave way to cooling sounds of Blue Grass and Memphis Blues. Water in the pool looked inviting but I thought better of it. Uncle Jessie drew a crowd just like when Momma and I watched him perform in outdoor cafes in Nashville. She was out of her dark place now and was a lot happier as she clapped and laughed along with the crowd.

My momma had a lot of self-control when called upon. A couple hours earlier she wasn't looking and tripped over an electrical cord. She got right up, brushed off her jeans, and looked around to see if anyone had noticed. She was safe, although I did laugh a little, just a little, to myself. She's even loveable when she's clumsy.

Did you ever hear Izzie sing? Oh my, I did love her, but even my ears couldn't take it. I, on the other hand, can still do a neat musical howl, good for a couple treats. I'm shocked to say it sometimes even worked on Mother Olivia.

I could tell by her laughter she thought Uncle Jessie was more interesting now that he had a trendy Nashville following. Back in my puppy years, I had a feeling Olivia secretly liked Jessie more than she acknowledged. Now that he's popular, she's more open with her interest. She told Izzie she had seen him at the Five-Spot, so she must have gone to Nashville more than we knew.

While Izzie listened to the music, I headed over to the cooking area and spotted Buddy. He'd chased a squirrel under the pile of lumber scraps. I set my eyes on some of the ladies, so I could do some tail wagging and make off with some tasty tidbits. Buddy gave up on the squirrel and followed my lead. Poor Buddy, sometimes he got mixed up on his duty in life. He thought his main responsibility was to catch a squirrel, which he did, one time, several years ago. Problem was, he didn't know what to do with it once he caught it. I knew my responsibility was to take care of Izzie. Did I mention she could trip over thin air?

Buddy and I spotted two women, both dressed in halter tops, one blue, one yellow, with tight-fitting white shorts. They were talking about Olivia as we sat at their feet listening to their gossip. We gave them the look-at-me stare. This is the expression that says these big eyes are begging for a treat. It worked. We ate our bits of meat and listened as the ladies patted our heads and continued to talk.

The one in the yellow top spoke in her Southern drawl. "Remember, when Olivia married Matt? She was so embarrassed that his brother Jessie managed a cock-fighting ring and was a country-folk singer. She was even more embarrassed after their Dad was murdered. Wasn't it then Jessie took over running their cock fighting, ahh, business?"

Blue Top hurriedly butted in, "Yes, and then Nashville heard of him. Before he was discovered you never saw Jessie here at any event, much less the annual barbeque. What a hunk he is. He's so handsome yet delicate in some way. Just enough grey hair to be distinguished yet rugged and all the women flirt with him."

"Did you know?" Yellow Top asked. "I heard Matt and Jessie's Mother had a total mental breakdown and never left her farmhouse after their dad's funeral. She sure would have been a mess if she'd lived long enough to see her son Matt die from the gun accident, or was it a homicide? I never heard the end of the unpleasant incident."

"You know, I'm not sure. The talk all over town soon became hush-hush and the whole story dropped out of the news. Izzie was so little. I wonder if she remembers any of what happened that day. She, Hannah, and Jake became wealthy children in a split second. Well, did you know, before I retired as loan officer at De Neal's State Bank there was a lot of talk? Real suspicious talk. I know for a fact that Jessie tried to borrow a large sum from Matt to set up his demo record. From then on things began to change. The brothers even had some arguments at the bank, behind closed doors, but I could hear them through a side door. Jessie seemed bitter toward Matt because of something, maybe restrictions put on the loan or maybe something more personal. Come to think of it, I don't believe that loan ever went through. I never heard the end because Matt died a few days later."

The women handed us carrot sticks, then sauntered over to the pool area where dripping wet swimmers where having sweet tea and beer. Carrots were not as great as the rib meat for the time we'd spent listening to such a long conversation. But, who knows, it never hurts to know the latest gossip even if it's old news. Those gals seemed to know a lot about this family. I recognized sweet tea 'cause it's always served in frosted glasses and onetime Hannah put a little bit in a bowl for me.

Meanwhile, Izzie, Jake, and Hannah mingled with all the guests until the fireworks started around nine o'clock. Buddy and I were too full to chase any cats or squirrels. The sound of those horrible fireworks rang in our ears, so we rested our fat tummies on the cool grass and sighed in shameless comfort. As the blasts of color disappeared from the sky, I smelled whiffs of rain. A summer storm was headed our way.

Late-night swimmers, filled with good food and good liquid, grabbed brightly colored towels and headed for the cabana. The fun and entertainment were over. From the laughter I heard, the guests enjoyed enough of each to be content until Olivia's Dog Daze party next year.

The sky, earlier draped with sparkly blasts of reds and blues, now had clouds that hung dark and threatening. I was ready to head home, or to the lodge. Buddy and I grabbed enough doggie treats to last awhile. Buddy hopped in Jake's Jeep, a nice juicy meat bone in his mouth. He wouldn't have it long when Jake saw him 'cause Buddy was not allowed bones. I would never have tried something so dumb, but what could I expect? He was a good pal, but not too bright and forgot his duty a lot of the time.

Chapter 6

The exterior light bulbs dimmed as Buddy and Jake headed to the lodge. The music had stopped. Everything was over except for the cleaning. My Sweetie turned to me and lovingly tugged on my ear.

"Let's go, Sammy. We'll have a night-cap with Jake. Wait, where's your leash?"

She hurried into the house with me two steps behind. It took Izzie enough time to find my leash for me to startle a mouse hugging the back wall of the pantry. He was guarding a morsel of dried crescent roll. I had just started to let him know who was boss of this kitchen when Izzie found my leash. Off we went. I hopped in the car, disappointed I was unable to finish the task at hand.

"We won't be missed. Mom's busy yacking with Uncle Jessie and Father Sims. They're helping her kill the last of the Drambuie. I'll bet Uncle Jessie will stay with Father Sims tonight. Those adoring crowds put him on a high and the Rusty Nails they were drinking should put him over the top. I bet you, my Love Sponge, Jessie sleeps this one off, as he usually does, at the welcomed hospitality of our good priest."

It started to sprinkle. My ears drooped, my body wilted as we hurried for the car. I was ready for some peaceful sleep. I turned at the sound of Hannah yelling for us to wait. Darn, what could she want? They'd both been at the party all evening.

"Mothers party was no fun without Patrick. I was miserable all evening, not seeing him. I really miss him. Do you think I should drive by his house, the one he now shares with only Guffin? Considering the turmoil of the day, don't you think he and his grandad would like some company?"

"Who are you kidding," Izzie answered. "You just want to see Patrick, comfort him as he has done for you since we were children."

"You're right, Izzie. I need to get to him. Oh, fiddlesticks. Now it's starting to rain, and I may have had a little too much whiskey and coke. Will you follow me over there?"

"You drive? I don't think so. I'll carry you over to Patrick's."

"Oh, come on. It's only a short mile there on a country road. I promise I'll go slow."

"Okay. Not a problem. Remember I warned you to be careful, it's against my better judgement."

Two jumps and I was in my doggie seat and ready to hit the road. We followed Hannah's car. The sprinkles suddenly turned to a thunderous downpour. I hate to get wet unless I'm getting a bath. That, I love. Even now at my mature age, when Izzie says bath time I run to the laundry room and wait to be lifted into the tub. In my youth I took delight jumping into the tub by myself.

We followed Hannah's car through the rainstorm as she drove toward Clarabelle and Guffin's clapboard house. Yellow shutters shone through the now blowing rain. I'm sure it was a reminder of Clarabelle and Guffin's gardening skills that brought tears to Izzie's eyes. To the right of the front door, down a moss-covered path, an arbor, hanging with honeysuckle provided a sweet fragrance I could smell even though the windows were up. The path led to the side doorway Patrick used for his entrance.

Most of the windows were dark and uninviting. One small window at the right side of the doorway was lit, the curtain open. Hannah turned off the engine of her Jag, hurriedly opened the car door, slammed it behind her and ran through the rain toward the light. The pathway led her to the man, I believed, she had loved since childhood.

Patrick must have heard the approaching car because he opened the door, waiting as she flew into his arms. I'm not sure, still it looked to me like she bit him. They went inside. I'd seen enough to know Hannah would not be going home tonight. Izzie put the car in reverse and slowly turned toward the road leading to the lodge.

Chapter 7

The deluge pelted our car. It was still hot and muggy at that late hour. I was riding along, listening to the rain hit the windshield, when Izzie slammed on the brakes, nearly throwing me out of my doggie seat. Mississippi mud splashed as high as the windows. She stopped in time for me to see Father Sims pull in front of us driving his old blue Dodge truck.

We were at a fork in the road. He had driven directly in front of us. Uncle Jessie, completely covered in his grey poncho followed, riding his pride and joy, a black Harley Davidson. I heard this name at the barbeque and thought it was the name of another entertainer until Buddy set me straight. He knew a lot about things that have motors. Though both vehicles were wet and muddy, they drove steadily, creeping through the black rainy night. We followed. Izzie drove just as carefully, perhaps having drank a few too many whiskeys herself.

We slowly pulled into Jake's driveway. Lights shone through the downstairs windows. As always, the lodge looked inviting. The stately Magnolias welcomed us as we approached the back door.

From my doggie seat in the back I could hear Izzie sniffling. I jumped in the front seat to have a peek. Yes, my sweetie looked sad. Her eyes were red and swollen as she stepped out of the Caddy and ran toward the kitchen door. The rainstorm turned to a light shower as suddenly as it appeared.

I rushed toward the inviting bushes. Buddy left me some wonderful smells. I grabbed a grape tomato off the vine. This is one of our favorite spots for peeing and stealing some home-grown tomatoes. As I bit down on one it popped juicy liquid and tiny seeds on my tongue. Yummy.

"Thanks for getting the door, Jake." Izzie's lower lip quivered. "Oh, Jake, so much has happened in one day. I'm exhausted. Mother's party was a success even with this cloud of sadness hanging over it. People there didn't love Clarabelle as we did. My heart is heavy. I always thought of her as my rainbow. Now I'm left with a storm."

"I understand. The whole family loved her." Jake wrapped his arms around Izzie's sobbing body. "Come join me. The shower has slowed to a sprinkle. Your suit is in the cabana. Let's take a relaxing swim, then call it a day and see what tomorrow brings. Should be a breeze after this one."

"Oh, yeah," I said to Buddy. "I think we have just begun." You see, I have a nose for such things. Buddy agreed, but I still have to watch out for him. You know, these Labs are very gullible.

Chapter 8

Jake's loud knock on the bedroom door woke us. I jumped out of bed, did a few downward dogs, and watched Izzie make herself ready for the day. The routine she formed when getting her nursing degree was with her all these years later.

She usually woke, jumped from the bed, landed on her feet, then typically tripped on her pajama leg, caught herself on the bedpost and took off to the bathroom. After ten minutes of stretches, she took a fast shower, put on her face of mascara and lipstick, dressed in jeans, top, and tennies. That day was different. She slid into a navy and white polka dot dress with shinny white sandals. I got in a few of my stretches as she brushed her shoulder-length hair. It took her thirty minutes in all, counting her stumbles.

She brushed her hair up into a ponytail. I finally got to go outside to do my duty. I moved a lot slower than Izzie. Those thirty minutes were not wasted on me. I found my Teddy Bear, gave him a good lick or two, then he watched me do my stretches as he always had. My morning routine was done much more leisurely and, I might add, in great form.

Have I told you about Izzie's hair? It flowed just past her shoulders, the color of a mud puddle after a heavy Mississippi rain. I guess it's about the color of Buddy, chocolate brown. When she pulled it back, little curls formed around her face and her neck. I looked at her hair and I was happy. It shone like the top of a lake, glimmering in the sun. My Grandog's coat did that. In my opinion it is a good thing to have a human's hair instead of a dog's. Human hair, at least, Izzie's, is soft, and always smelled like a forest after a cool rain. I've had a nose for such things ever since I was a puppy.

Because we were staying at Jake's, I'd anticipated this would be a fun day. He cooked a mean breakfast. Buddy and I always got a whole slice of bacon which we ate outside the kitchen door. The door, screened in to keep out pesky flies, led to the covered veranda which led to the pool, one of our favorite places to play catch. The sun was out today, and I'd hoped we'd chase each other around the pool for some fun.

Buddy was so gentle he could carry an egg in his mouth and not crack it. This was just one of the tricks Jake taught him. I, on the other hand, preferred to eat the egg, scrambled or boiled, then do a trick, if required.

Buddy and I had this game we played to keep our swimming skills in top shape. He dropped the plastic fish into the pool at one end. I jumped in, swam to his end and retrieved it. I would climb out while he ran to the opposite end. I dropped the fish, Buddy jumped in, swam to my end and so on. We were exhausted when this game was over. We always needed a nap on the veranda to recover.

While we were playing, Izzie finished her poached eggs on toast, cantaloupe, and steamy black coffee. Among other things, Izzie and Jake shared their love of aromatic roasted coffee. Funny thing, I knew people pressed their clothes, but it was new to me when Jake said he needed to French Press his coffee.

He told Izzie last Easter when we were visiting, he'd ordered these little green beans from some place called Costa Rica. One time I discovered some that had tumbled out of an old burlap bag. I found them to be hard as a rock and not very good to chew. Anyway, I heard Jake tell Izzie he takes them to someplace in Memphis. They come back all black and oily. One morning, while making her coffee, Izzie said these roasted beans were wonderful. This made no sense to me. Humans are sometimes strange. I prefer steak, raw if you please.

Chapter 9

Buddy and I were deep into our morning naptime. We jumped at the sound of Izzie and Jake closing the veranda screen door. They had left without us.

"Let's go, Jake. We'll be late for Mass. Maybe we'll stay for coffee and donuts, what do you think?"

We were disappointed to learn that today would be a stay-at-home day for us. But on the bright side, with them gone a few hours, I would have time to play with Buddy. We played, ate, and slept a lot. After several chases around the pool we had time for a nap. I dozed and had my reoccurring dream about the time when I was a puppy and rolled in the horse manure. I remembered the squishiness as I rolled in it. I had been a smelly mess. My daydream was shattered by the slam of the back door. Izzie and Jake were home.

Taking two steps at a time, Izzie bounded upstairs. I followed as fast as a Shih Tzu can run which is fast for these short legs. She changed into a crisp white shirt and jeans with red tennies she calls Keds.

Izzie yelled down the stairs, "Jake, I'm ready to go when you are."

The word "go" was like a flash of information to us, a clue for Buddy and me to race as fast as we could toward the back door. We seldom knew where we were going, but we'd bum a ride no matter where they took us.

My problem with car trips was the way Buddy tried to hang his head out the window. His slobbers always flew back and hit me in the face. Man, he had bad breath. This time Buddy was content to lay in the back seat as Jake drove. We got to Clarabelle's house as Patrick and Hannah were coming outside.

"Patrick, where's your grandad? Is his leg acting up today?" Izzie quizzed.

"Yes, he's in a bad way this morning. You know, he'd had seasons on the circuit, then one tumble off that bronco ten years ago left him with nothing but a busted hip and plenty of belt buckles." Patrick ran his hands through his hair. "The police just left. They wanted a final look around, asked a few questions and even took some of his prize buckles off the wall before they cleared the scene. It seems the coroner wasn't sure it was a heart attack. They're probably overthinking, but they hesitated when I asked why they were questioning Grandmother's death."

"That makes no sense at all. Everyone in town knew she had heart trouble. You said yourself that she looked like she had just gone to sleep. Where'd the coroner come up with such an idea?" Izzie laid her hand on Patrick's arm. "Do you still want us to go through her things today or wait until later?"

"Yes, please go ahead," Patrick said. "They've cleared the house. Clean out some of Grandmother's more conspicuous items so Guffin doesn't see reminders of her in every room. Jake, if you would come with grandad and me to the coroner's office we could let the gals get started. I have several questions I want to ask about his findings."

"But this is Sunday," Izzie said.

"I know, but he said he would be working a couple hours between noon and two o'clock. We want to catch him before he leaves."

Jake scratched Buddy's ear. "Ready when you are. Buddy, you stay here with Izzie. Here comes Guffin. I'll drive. Later, ladies." Jake gave us a thumbs-up as the three fellows got in Jake's black Jeep.

Jake was right. Buddy needed to stay here with me. Clarabelle's passing caused me to think really deep. We had some sniffing to do, then work out a plan to let Izzie know everything we suspected pertaining to Clarabelle's death. We were up for a huge challenge.

"Let's get started," said Izzie. "I need to get home this afternoon to clean the boat and I have to be at the hospital for my shift at six-thirty in the morning. Unfortunately, I didn't get a chance yesterday to clean any of the mess we girls made before I headed down here."

"Did I miss a party last week?" Hannah asked.

"Some of the nurses from St Jude's came to the boat for drinks Friday night and we left things in a mess. I had planned to spend Saturday morning cleaning the boat then come down here in the afternoon for Mom's party. When I got the urgent call from Jake, I drove down as soon as I could."

"Works for me. What day are you coming back?" said Hannah.

"Either Wednesday or Thursday. I'll know as soon as they set the day of the funeral."

Okay, let's get started."

Chapter 10

Izzie followed Hannah as she opened the front screen door and stepped into the entry room. They walked into the living area, Hannah's hands on her hips. They looked down a hallway which led into the small kitchen and pantry. I knew this house 'cause I'd been here many times in my formative years.

"There's not too much of a mess except for the area around her chair." Hannah looked around. "Clarabelle ran Mother's home just like her own." Stepping in the kitchen she stopped. "Even the groceries are arranged in the same order."

"I'll start in the bedroom and bath," yelled Izzie, already going down the short hall to her right.

The linoleum flooring, printed in squares of tan and cream, provided a cool surface for me and Buddy to rest our furry, warm bodies. Also, from that point we could hear everything the sisters said. That was if we could stay awake. Buddy groaned, not in the least bit interested in what Hannah had to say. Keen as I was about gossip, my ears were in alert mode and taking in every word.

Noticing the braided living room rug hanging on the back-porch railing, Hannah checked to see if it was dry and carried it into the living room.

"Hey, Izzie, the coke stain has been washed off the rug, will you help me put it back under Clarabelle's chair and side table?"

"Sure, did the stain come out?" Izzie asked, coming out of the bathroom. "Here, let me move the side table."

Izzie reached to pick up the small oak table. A coke bottle and two bottle caps fell on the floor. She picked them up, noticed another coke bottle under the chair. Then she pitched all without comment in the waste basket nearby.

"There, that looks better. Now I'll tilt the chair and you can spread out the rug.

Going back to the bedroom, the girls found several aprons folded neatly in an old hickory rocker. They put the aprons on the tall bookshelf Clarabelle used as a storage unit. All her other items were folded or in baskets. The girls talked as they worked. Izzie said Clarabelle had a flair for decorating in her organized way.

"Shall we change the sheets on the twin beds while we are here?" asked Hannah.

"Why not? It will be better for Guffin if we do as much as possible. The laundry can be washing while we check the second bathroom and finish in the living room," said Hannah. "No need to check Patrick's room. I left it neat as a pin."

Hannah removed the sheets and pillowcases from Guffin's bed. Then she headed toward the small laundry room which was actually a large closet that held a wooden ironing board, one laundry basket, and two machines. One single light bulb hung from the ceiling providing the only hint of light.

Izzie followed her, "Something's strange here."

"What do you mean?"

"Well, Clarabelle was very particular with the way she maintained her house, how she folded her sheets and pillowcases in her linen closet. But there was no pillowcase covering the pillow on her bed. Knowing Clarabelle, it would've matched the one on Griffin's bed. It was the one with the pretty lavender tatting. Don't you think that's strange, one pillow with a case and the other without?"

"Not really, maybe she had used it for something, and we'll find it in the laundry basket."

While Hannah moved the ironing board to the side and dumped something white and fluffy from a box to the washer, Izzie dropped the items from the laundry basket into the washer piece by piece. That was odd.

No pillowcase.

Chapter 11

"It seems odd the funeral was postponed until today." Izzie said as she opened the car door.

Nearly two weeks had passed since cleaning day at Clarabelle's. It was another sticky, humid summer day.

Buddy and I panted but were dog-happy by the time we jumped into Jake's air-conditioned Jeep. Izzie said we were on a short ride to the church for Clarabelle's funeral mass. It's so close to the lodge we could've run there but that ride was much cooler. Izzie talked as Jake drove down the lane toward the hard road.

"Do you think there's still a question concerning Clarabelle's death?"

"Possibly."

"Do you think the coroner suspects a different cause of death than a heart attack?"

"Well, remember the Sunday Patrick, Guffin, and I met with the coroner? Based on their joint experience, he as a coroner for twenty-five years and Patrick as a doctor, they discussed several unusual observations that would not be attributed to a heart attack. Coroner

Gaskins told Patrick the first thing he observed when Dr. Daut called him to come to issue the death certificate was blood had oozed from Clarabelle's mouth. That is unusual for a heart attack. Also, her eyes were bloodshot."

"Several conditions could cause that to happen," said Izzie.

"Yes, I realize that. However, cyanosis of the skin was also apparent. It's caused by a lack of oxygen in the blood. That bluish skin discoloration even on a person of color would indicate a lack of oxygen to the body."

"You're right, I've seen this when working ER."

"Also, though slight, he detected the skin pale around the mouth and nose which you know can mean pressure was applied to the face which could have been caused by smothering. So, with those observations, he was required by law to contact the Medical Examiner who would require the County Pathologist to do an autopsy."

"When do you think Patrick will hear?

"Any time now."

Izzie rode the rest of the way to the church in complete silence, arms crossed. Frequently she rubbed the nape of her neck.

I, on the other hand, tried to remember what Izzie had said about her phone call with Clarabelle the week or two before she died. Something she said about Guffin cussing, storming out of the house when Clarabelle questioned him about his late-night gambling. Probably nothing.

We were among the first to arrive for the funeral mass. Family members and a handful of others were scattered throughout the church. Olivia, Hannah, Izzie, Jake, and Uncle Rocco sat on the left with mass books open. The black and yellow checked suit Olivia wore fit her like a glove. Had it not been for the bright yellow silk flower at her bust line she would've looked lovely. She should have worn a black flower or none at all.

Grief and a feeling of loss were expressed in the tailored black suits worn by Izzie and Hannah. Jake extended his arm around the back of the pew to pat Izzie on the shoulder. He rubbed his black beard with his other hand as he stared at the altar. I studied Uncle Rocco. He was a handsome Italian man but today worry lines covered his forehead as he stroked his salt and pepper beard.

Some might wonder why Buddy and I were there, so we stayed in the back, keeping a low profile which was hardly called for because we, or at least I, was one of Clarabelle's dearest friends and confidants. We shared some good times, watching Perry Mason reruns, solving the crimes. I learned a lot about clues from Clarabelle. She explained the stories over and over.

Alone in the front right pew sat Patrick, his grandfather, Guffin, and Patrick's mother. Patrick sat erect and solemn faced. He wore a grey pin-striped suit over a black silk crew neck shirt. Guffin's black suit hung, drooped over his bowed body. He gave in to bouts of sobbing and trembling. Patrick's mother, Clarabelle and Guffin's only child, tried to comfort her father as she wept.

The casket, covered with what looked like a white dining-room tablecloth and an X made of wood, was pushed down the aisle by six men with serious faces. The procession was led by the priest to the altar adorned in white lilies and camellias. Catholic funerals are long, solemn ceremonies punctuated with mournful music. When Uncle Jessie sang Nearer My God to Thee and Ava Maria I saw several people blowing their noses. I never knew there could be so many people with colds in the heat of July.

After mass, Clarabelle's coffin was lowered in a deep hole in the ground behind the little church. I was sure there was a lot of sadness or colds because many people still dabbed their noses. After the hole dropping ceremony, Buddy and I followed Jake and Izzie to the basement of the church where a meal, furnished by ladies of the church, was served. The basement was a gathering place where parties and bingos were held. A kitchen, storage area, and general catch-all room completed the floor plan. Over the years, at one event or another, Buddy and I had chased several mice in that catch-all room, never with any positive results.

Following the blessing of the food, Father Sims sat with Uncle Jessie. It was a great smelling funeral meal. Juicy baked ham provided Buddy and me with tasty hand-outs. However, the green beans made us beg for more. I'm sure I could taste bacon seasoning in them.

Even on this sad occasion Buddy and I had something to be thankful for. We decided to settle under the table shared by Father Sims and Uncle Jessie. While we enjoyed those tasty green beans, some discussion from above began to hold our interest. Buddy stopped chewing and tilted his head.

Most of the mourners gave their condolences and left after eating. Izzie and Jake, who were engaged in conversation with Uncle Rocco, continued to visit. Long ago Mommadog told me he is not a real blood relative uncle, but after Matt's death he was a support to Olivia for the girls and especially for Jake who was eighteen.

She also told me years earlier Mr. Gianni Rocco had hired eighteen-year-old Matt to work for his construction company in Memphis. Matt wanted to leave Caruthersville with Janice, his young wife. The offer from Rocco to work in his company in Memphis was good for Matt, not so good for his young wife. They divorced two years later, six months after Jake was born.

Patrick and Guffin stood to leave. Father Sims noticed and hurried over to them and did the hand shaking thing humans do. I think it's like the tail-sniffing greeting we dogs do. I can learn a lot about a dog by those sniffs. After saying goodbye to the remaining mourners, Father Sims again joined Jessie. The priest was frowning and seemed, as I've heard humans say, to have the weight of the world on his shoulders.

Too much food. Buddy's eyes were drooping. I stayed alert.

The priest pulled out a chair, sat, and turned to Jessie. "As you may remember, we talked the day before the barbeque about Clarabelle. I'm afraid I may have revealed too much information from her confession."

"Yeah, sure, I remember. I'd come down from Memphis to practice with the band the night before the party. You were in a talking mood, for sure."

"Clarabelle talked to me in great detail in her weekly confession a few days before she died. She wanted absolution for things she knew that were weighing on her mind. I had no thought she would be gone so soon."

"Sometimes the heart just gives out," replied Jessie in a tone that seemed more sarcastic than concerned.

My smeller started to work overtime. The hair started to rise on my back. Jessie was sweating. I could smell the anger coming from him. I looked up and caught a glimpse of Jessie's flushed face, his raised eyebrows.

Father Sims' shoulders slumped and with a tired expression, he began talking about the past, perhaps knowing he too was dying, I suspected, of that lung thing I had heard Izzie mention.

Still engaged in conversation with Rocco, Izzie and Jake paid no attention to us dogs. Buddy and I stayed quietly under the table, listening, and smelling. Suddenly Buddies eyes widened, and my ears perked.

"You know this cancer is terminal, I must confess my guilt to the Bishop," Father Sims blurted.

"I know nothing of the kind," uttered Jessie. "You aren't guilty of anything. What are you thinking? You were just helping a friend. God understands what we did. You knew at the time I couldn't let that kid get away with killing my Pa. You knew it was necessary. I had to vindicate Big Ed." Jessie's voice had gone high-pitched.

"No killing is ever warranted, we should have let the authorities handle it."

"Authorities? That Spencer kid's pa was a deputy Sheriff. Do you honestly believe they'd have brought him to trial? I think you've forgotten how t'was back in those times."

"I remember like it was yesterday." Father Sims sighed.

Buddy's snoring got louder as I leaned against his back. My eyelids were heavy, but I heard Jessie say, "I remember the incident as well as you, Father. Your Ram truck was new and shiny then. You pulled up toward the weather-beaten barn on the Old Spencer Place and my pa came out ta greet ya.

"Big Eddy had yelled on that night long ago, "Hi there, Padre. You'll get a thrill with tonight's fights. Yes, ya will. These cocks of mine should be the big winners. This here event will have some good wagers. The stakes are high. Come on in and win ya self some money.

"Around the cockpit was a frenzy of activity," said Jessie. "The blood sport was spurred on by drunken ne'er-do-wells and high rollers from Memphis. I remember Mr. Rocco, one of the weekly regulars, played for big stakes. They had little on their minds except an evening of cussin', screamin', blood and guts."

"It was after the final cockfight of the night that another fight ensued that caused our problem," said the priest.

"Yah, my pa was leaving through the weathered back door when he was approached by young Willy Spencer, knife in hand, and enough booze under his belt to ensure the evening was not entirely over."

"I remember their conversation," said Father. '"Hey, ya old fart.' Willy yelled at Big Eddy."

"Ya a-talkin to me, ya young smart ass?

"Sho am. You took two-thousand dollars from me in those last two fuckin' fights with that juiced up cock of yours. Nobody gets away with that. My Pa taught me to take care of those who screw around with us Spencer's.'"

Jessie's voice was loud, "I heard the yelling. Ran out behind Pa in time to see the end of a drunken brawl leaving Big Eddy on the brown dusty ground, grasping his belly, red blood gushing between his fingers. Unnoticed by the Spencer kid, you, Father, stepped out of the woods where you had relieved yourself and witnessed the stabbing. We saw the kid stagger as he was running into the woods. Running to Big Ed, you knelt in the dirt and held my Pa as he wrenched in pain. I was close enough to hear you mutter, 'the whiskey devil led Willy astray.'"

"I only did what any priest would have done."

"Then," continued Jessie, "with an angry fire burning in my gut, I ran into the woods after Willy. The woods were dense. I tripped over a tree root but kept going, sweat nearly blinding my eyes. I caught up to the kid as he slid down into the muddy riverbank. When you caught up with me, it was too late. I was at the river's edge, knife in hand, vomit covering my blood-stained bib overalls." Jessie rambled on, "You held my Father, a poor man you loved despite his weaknesses. You gave him absolution. We are the only ones who know what happened to Willy Spencer before his stabbed and mangled body washed up on the riverbank two weeks later. We are the only ones who know why both his hands had been severed."

"I've played that scene over and over in my head. So many years have passed but I still can't forgive myself," interrupted Father Sims.

Veins in Jessie's neck pulsated as he pushed back the chair so hard it skidded across the floor. "We'll talk about this later. I doubt the Bishop can save your soul at this late date. I'll be by the rectory later on."

With that he hurriedly went up the basement stairs leaving Father Sims staring in disbelief at the outburst of his friend.

I wasn't sure what had just happened. Jessie stomped up the stairway leading to the vestibule. Izzie, Jake, and Uncle Rocco stood to leave. Buddy followed my lead and we hurried after them. We'd heard plenty. Time to move on and think about the story we had just heard. Or, had I been dreaming?

Chapter 12

In the middle of a wild, senseless doggie dream I was jarred awake. I'd been dreaming those barn cats were skunks. Maybe they were skunks. They did fart a lot. What woke me?

Was it the sound of Izzie's outrageous snoring? No, I was hearing the blaring sirens of firetrucks. They were in the distance but the shrill was getting closer and louder. Years ago, in my puppy years, I was fetching my favorite green ball from the gutter. Then one of those big trucks came blaring toward me. I was so scared I peed right there without a bush.

I got testy when I heard shrill sounds. I held my paws over my ears. No help. Next, I pawed at Izzie's back. She didn't stir. I pawed at her back again. No response. I waited, then pawed at her hair. I couldn't believe she wasn't hearing that piercing sound.

Time to act. I dug at the sheet, got it in a kind of knot, bit down on it with a tight grip and started pulling. I was able to jerk it from her body but then she just yanked it up around her neck. I tugged again, this time with all my strength. Finally, I got a response. She moved.

"Okay, little Love Sponge, what's the problem?" Izzie yawned and stretched.

I stared at her with wide eyes and cocked head. She immediately sat up in bed. I waited. Then I did the only thing I could think of. I jumped off the bed, ran to the window, barked my loudest bark ever, gave her my cocked head expression. It worked.

"Is that a siren I hear?" she jumped from the bed and ran bare foot on the wood floor. Tripping on my fuzzy turtle, she caught herself on the bedpost, steadied herself, and ran toward the window.

Izzie occasionally took refuge from the world in the room where we stayed at Jake's house. As she grew into adulthood it was her space away from her mother's house and the bouts of drinking she often witnessed there.

The room was in Jake's home, but we claimed that part of the house as our own. I had fun staying there. Unlike the home of Mother Olivia, Izzie's room here had a lot of stuff for me to investigate. My toys could be all over the floor and no one cared, except when they tripped over them. That could be often where Izzie was concerned. At least I didn't leave wet and slobbery half-chewed bones on the floor, like Buddy. I hid mine.

Izzie grabbed her pastel silk robe and yelled for Jake to wake up as she ran down the stairs.

Jake rubbed his eyes. "Where's the fire?"

"Look out back, beyond the soybean field. To the right of the cabana. Looks like a bright light coming from the church. We'd better get dressed and investigate. I'll be ready in a minute." Izzie ran upstairs.

It was dark out, too early for the sun. Did we have to go now?

Jake drove us toward the church. Buddy's nose poked out the window hiding most of the view from me. When we got closer, Buddy moved over to give me a look. Flames leaped from two windows on the right side of the massive double front doors. Policemen kept us out of the way as firemen worked to put out the fire. I wanted to know more, but we had to get in the car and leave for Memphis. At the first break of dawn Izzie usually left for her ER shift. That was typically after my trip to Jake's glorious holly bushes. Somehow in the confusion of that morning, I didn't get my walk to those bushes.

I was thinking Izzie had better drive fast. The courtyard awaited.

Chapter 13

Izzie rubbed the nape of her neck as she drove. Movement like that told me she was in her dark, silent place. The drive north to Memphis was fast and quiet. Home at last. I bounced out of the car and ran to the courtyard where we met Little Daisy and I answered nature's call. I felt like a new dog as we stepped into the elevator. Daisy's owner, Mr. Cohen, a fat gentleman who constantly popped his suspenders held the door for us. He and Izzie planned a playdate for Daisy and me.

Back at the loft, Izzie filled my water dish and hurried into the bedroom to change into those things she calls scrubs. That's also the name of what she says before my bath. When she popped me in the bathtub she always asked if I wanted a good scrubbing. I was confused when she also said she was wearing them to work. I guess I should have remembered that people were a bit strange and accepted the fact that I never did understand everything Izzie did.

I slept most of the day Friday while she was at work except for a little watching of Perry Mason. She called it a double shift. We had a quiet evening at home while Izzie unpacked her suitcase and I got a late-night walk toward the wharf at President's Island. Saturday was a repeat of the day before, except I got my playdate with Daisy. For a Shih Tzu, Daisy was one picky eater. She took every bite Mr. Cohen put in her bowl, carried it to the mat by the kitchen door and ate it there. Pretty as she was, that dog made me love people even more. At least they sat still and ate off their plates, which is good for me. I could gobble up any morsel dropped on the floor before Daisy would decide what to do with it.

Daisy snatched her funny monkey, the toy with one arm missing, from her toy basket and wanted me to chase her which, of course, I did. I made sure I didn't catch her, or she'd want to stop playing. When I jumped on Izzie's bed that night, I was exhausted from my play-day.

I planned to sleep the whole morning until nature called. It had been two days since we were awakened by the piercing sound of the fire engines. I was wrong again. It was not a typical Saturday morning like I'd expected. The phone rang and Izzie grabbed it on the second ring. My nature call had to wait. I heard Jake's voice when My Sweetie pressed the speaker button on the phone.

"The church fire was devastating. It burned much of the basement and some of the first floor on the right above the kitchen," Jake said. "Chief Hensley thinks the fire started in the basement kitchen area. Father Sims, understandably, will be overwhelmed by the catastrophe.

"Today is the first day anyone will be allowed inside the rubble. If you are free, why not drive down and we'll check it out? Perhaps Father Sims will be back at the rectory by then and we can visit with him."

My eyeballs were floating, meaning my bladder was about to explode. Nature called me, but Izzie didn't hear. She tripped over my green turtle in her hurry, then spilled the coffee she'd put by the front door for the drive. What a morning. I was finally able to take care of my needs in the courtyard. We entered the underground garage as Sabbath darted in front of Izzie. The coffee spilled down the front on her shirt didn't detain her. We started our drive on I-55 south to Nesbit.

"That church held many memories for me." She pulled out of the underground garage. "Let's try to have a word with Father if we find him at the rectory."

Driving toward Nesbit was like reliving the past.

"Hey, Love Sponge, shall we go by the rectory, then straight to the church, or what's left of it? Jake said he'd meet us there after he finished some work at the barn."

The trees whizzed by as we headed south. Oh, how I longed to stick my nose out the window. Izzie left me in my doggie seat and knocked on the door of the rectory but got no response. Taking a glance at the carport I realized she wouldn't get a reply since the truck was gone. My momma looked disappointed as she walked toward to car to get me.

"I guess Father Sims isn't home. Oh well, let's walk over to the ruins."

Izzie opened the back door and I hopped out of the back seat ready to start my investigation. She walked toward the church, I trotted close behind until we got to the front steps.

My nose twitched as I caught a whiff of something repugnant. Memories of the dead possum Buddy and I stumbled upon behind the old barn filled my brain. I didn't like the odor coming from in there and the fragments of ash and debris would make me dirty, so I stayed outside.

I laid on the top step, my head resting between my paws. The steps led to what used to be the front door of St. Mary's Church. A part of the front and down the left side of the church burned and was in ruin, but the altar and kneeling rails at the front were hardly charred.

The hand-stenciled vestibule walls leading to the basement were covered in smoke. A mess of broken beams and plaster scattered over the once beautiful mosaic floor. The basement was roped off. Voices came from the lower area. Izzie walked around the piles of debris. Where was she going?

Chapter 14

She walked toward the front of the church, then knelt as if in prayer. Knowing her as only I did, I figured she wasn't praying. She was angry. She could have been talking to God or anyone who might have been listening. I always listened.

I left my place on the top step and followed Izzie close enough to hear. "Why would anyone burn this beautiful church?" I jumped into the pew beside her. She was abruptly quiet for a few minutes as she patted my head. I felt warm from the bright sunlight coming through the chapel window. She squinted in the sunlight.

"Some things are easy to remember. What a funny and jovial patron of our soul Father Timothy Sims was. He made the grouchy nuns smile when he told religious jokes. His reassignment here under circumstances that were a disgrace to his parish in Caruthersville, Missouri was a godsend for this parish."

She was still kneeling as she stopped patting my head and scratched my right ear.

"It became known that Father Sims had inherited a vast sum of money when his parents died. This inheritance allowed him to upgrade the

Church and Rectory before he was transferred. Did he pay for hidden guilt or did he want to be generous with his wealth?"

Izzie was talking out loud but to herself. I sat erect, cocked my head to listen but choose not to answer.

"His only personal indulgence had been the purchase of a new, bright blue Dodge Ram truck. The inheritance also allowed him to wager heavily on illegal cockfights held every Thursday night at the Old Spencer Place."

Mommadog told this story several times when we eave-dropped on cocktail party conversations. I felt sure everything she'd said was true. Buddy had also filled me in on a couple of details about Jessie and the good priest.

"Enough of childhood memories."

Izzie slowly stood as the sunshine flashed through the stained-glass window resting on her ponytail. I saw a kaleidoscope of color, red color, on the floor of the Church. I was reminded of the story Izzie told me of that horrible night her daddy was killed. She rubbed the nape of her neck, then her eyes.

My desire to comfort her made me quiver. I could only lick her hand to remind her of my devotion.

Sweet Momma gripped the pew as she stood. She stepped into the aisle. She stopped, gently kicked the ashes, and stepped over the burnt rubble as a young mother would tip toe through the nursery of her first-born child.

By the frowned expression on her face, Izzie was remembering something from her childhood, maybe about her daddy, Matt. Shoulders slumped, she did not move. "Sammy, I just remembered Daddy gave me my dolly with the red dress. The highlight of my birthday was opening the box, tearing away the tissue paper and seeing her pretty face and the red taffeta dress."

• • •

Grandog told Mommadog about that day, now some twenty years ago. Izzie had just celebrated her sixth birthday the week before with colored balloons, red and white streamers, friends, family, and her beloved puppy, Grandog Stella.

That morning, like every other day, had started in the church. More obedient girls than Izzie, in uniforms nicely starched, followed the prayers being recited by the teaching nuns. Those girls believed their prayers would put them in the grace with God. Young Izzie made her peace with God more hurriedly than the others.

Mommadog said Izzie's girlish laughter could be heard above the mummer of the rosary being said by the Sisters of the Immaculate Heart. She had little concern that her white blouse was not tucked neatly into her navy skirt nor that her knees were scraped from tripping up the church stairs. She and her group stayed in the back pews. She used this time of prayer to tell her latest imaginary escapades to the other uniformed students who were beguiled by her and without hesitation listened to her stories.

The nuns took notice of these transgressions. Parents were called to the Academy. Little changed.

Granted, the church was not the place for storytelling. It did, however, add to the thrill of the moment with the mummer of prayers in the foreground. To Izzie, the sound of prayer had been the perfect accompaniment to her colorful stories. That day, too, the bright sunlight came through the stained-glass windows—a prism of color on the floor.

Izzie trembled as she leaned down toward the pew where I lay. She absent-mindedly scratched my ear. Her voice was a soft whisper.

"I had gone home after school thinking how much I enjoyed those days at the Academy. Clarabelle and little Stella greeted me at the side door of the kitchen. Clarabelle was pickling beets and had just cleaned a chicken for dinner. It was wonderful to have a grownup friend to tell about the day. After my visit with Clarabelle over a cool glass of lemonade, I took Stella and some toys to the library to play.

"Daddy was in his office. He had not hunted since the accident a couple years before, but he still told me exciting stories about those days. He wheeled around in his wheelchair to look the other way, pretended not to see me. When he was alone, I would bring my dolls, toys, and go to my hiding place behind the black leather sofa. Stella and I would play and listen to Daddy's stories. Occasionally I peeked around the sofa to get a glimpse of him."

Mommadog told me Izzie's daddy was telling her another hunting story. It was a day like so many others. Days with Daddy Matt were special to Izzie. She could play behind the sofa, her special hideaway. He knew she was there although she could not be seen from the doorway nor from behind his desk. Mommadog said Clarabelle told her Matt adored his youngest daughter, and this was his special time with her.

Matt would work on estimates for the next construction bid or clean his guns, talking about adventures he's experienced. He would never acknowledge she was in the room but would talk into the thin air, amused by her giggles. Her favorite dolly, in a pretty red dress, with hair ribbons either missing or in disarray, also listened to his stories. The mummer of his voice was soothing, and Little Izzie listened as she drifted into his world, reliving his adventures.

One day, after I rolled in the horse poop, Clarabelle gave me a scrubby bath. She was in one of her talking-about-the-past moods and told me something else. Izzie's father told stories of his youth as the oldest son of a Mississippi sharecropper. His younger brother, Jessie, preferred to stay on the farm, work the cockfights. Matt had bigger plans. He was a newly married teenager when he and his first wife, Jake's Mother, moved to Memphis to work for Mr. Rocco, Mr. Rocco was one of the weekly game cock gamblers who owned a commercial construction company in Memphis."

Clarabelle scrubbed me twice before I was clean. Horse poop is not easy to remove from a Shih Tzu's silky coat.

"Matt applied himself, was a fast learner and soon became a project manager at Gianni Rocco Construction Company," Clarabelle said. "Janice hated Memphis. After two years of marriage she took their six-month old son, Jake, and moved back to Caruthersville. Rocco remained friends with both his employee, now his protégé, as well as Janice, the ex-wife. Matt's stories of how he worked to overcome the "poor trash" label impressed young Izzie, as it had Mr. Rocco years earlier."

Clarabelle dried my coat with Izzie's powerful hair dryer as she told me more about the family she worked for and loved.

"As a single man for many years Matt acquired property and wealth. With his second marriage to Izzie's mother, Olivia, the world was his oyster. With this accomplishment came the best stories of all—his stories of Hannah, the older sister, of Izzie when she was a baby, and those of big game expeditions in faraway exotic places."

Olivia had never gone on these adventures. Perhaps Matt found some greater peace in those trips since she did not share them. Izzie was sure she would go with him some day when she became a teenager. She could hardly wait for that day. Such endearing memories.

Then, in a sudden, bright flash, her world had changed.

Back at the church, Izzie turned to walk out through the rubble. Then she stopped, picked me up in her arms, and stroked my fur. She told me how, as a little girl, she sat cross-legged in Matt's office behind the black sofa.

"That day had seemed different somehow. Sammy, I don't know why, just different. Perhaps daddy's voice was strained."

Perhaps Izzie knew her daddy too well.

I listened intently to Izzie, my eyes glued on her bottom lip as it jutted out.

"The dollies were being good that day and listened to Daddy's story.

They sat prim and proper as Momma said I should do. They sat like my big sister Hannah, always paying attention. Hannah was never lost in this world of "special places". Hannah never liked Daddy's stories, but I, with my dollies and Stella, loved to listen as his low melodic voice spin tales of adventure.

"The glaring sunlight blasted through the library window. I spied my kaleidoscope by the leg of the black sofa. A gift from Uncle Rocco the week before on my sixth birthday. He was just a close family friend who was called "Uncle." A favorite gift from my favorite Uncle. Spellbound, I watched the dazzling colors in this sphere of color. Meant just for me, like the special rainbow Daddy had shown me the day before, after a spring rain."

"Pieces of glass fell into place as I held the kaleidoscope to my eye. Turning toward the large window behind the sofa the colors in the cylinder took on more brilliance. Lost in the spell of the moment, I turned the cylinder slowly in my small hand. Daddy was telling about his hunt for the big elk that hung behind his massive desk."

What happened next? The adult, Izzie, tried to step back. She tried to remember. Those vague recollections were like the debris in the burnt chapel. She drifted in and out of her dark place.

Izzie held me tightly next to her. I felt her tense body. She carried me toward the entrance. My Sweet Momma staggered as she tripped on a pile of charred plaster. She steadied herself and we walked away from the church on that sweltering day.

I knew what had happened. I knew because my world wasn't in a daze. My world was clear. When I thought of my sweetie, my mind was always clear. That day in the burnt church Izzie had tried to step back. The church was a burnt tomb to her. She tried to remember. Her elusive memories were like the rubble in the burnt church.

Each time dear Izzie tried to pick up a memory, it turned to ash.

Chapter 15

I had a restless night. You probably know the kind. It's when you go around in circles, then more circles to get the right feeling of the bed.

The trouble started when Izzie and I decided to sleep-over at Mother Olivia's. As the evening progressed our plans changed. Plans got changed a lot, especially in that family. My head was still in a swirl the next morning, perhaps in a bit of a daze.

Hannah was still staying at Olivia's since the Dog Daze Party, the funeral, and her usual summer break. Most of her other time was spent with Patrick, in Nashville. He was a Hematologist and Professor at Meharry Medical School where he specialized in sickle cell anemia. Hannah was a coordinator for the same University's Community Health Center. Because she spoke Spanish, Creole, and French, her service was well used and appreciated. Their relationship was something everyone knew about, but no one discussed.

When the couple was in Nesbit, Patrick always stayed with his grandparents, Clarabelle and Guffin. Hannah stayed with Olivia, thereby eliminating a lot of small-town talk.

Dinner the night before of filet mignon and asparagus was great for me, not so great for dear Izzie and Hannah. Mother Olivia had started the evening much too early with very dry gin martinis. I know they were dry because when she spilled her third one on the carpet, I only got a whiff of vermouth when I grabbed the olive. She followed at dinner with something she called a merlot. I'm not sure what it was, but it was red, and if you drank the whole bottle you could talk a lot faster and louder.

Conversation centered on the absence of Father Sims. He had not been heard from since the fire, yet no one seemed to remember him mentioning a plan to be gone.

Olivia said, "My call earlier today to Jessie revealed no information. Jessie said when he left the rectory the evening before the fire there had been no mention of a plan to take a trip."

Olivia was in one of her disgusting moods. She's like that when she drinks and talks, drinks more, and talks louder. Not a good combination where that woman is concerned.

Tired from the day, Izzie and I retreated upstairs to go to bed about nine o'clock as Olivia reached for her after-dinner Drambuie Liquor. Hannah was caught, she could not escape. Her Mother was letting the red stuff, the merlot, and now the Drambuie, do the talking.

A short time later my bladder twinged. Two sharp barks told Izzie I had to piddle. She had been in such a hurry to get away from the conversation she had forgotten to let me have my late-night nature call. Down the stairs I ran and headed for the front door.

Izzie was two steps behind me.

"He attacked me." Olivia screeched. "Didn't you hear me? That son of a bitch father of yours raped me. How in the hell did you think Izzie got here? It sure wasn't by mutual consent."

Izzie stopped abruptly.

"What are you talking about?" Hannah loudly questioned.

I could hear the tears in her voice. "Daddy couldn't do such a thing."

"Oh, no? You don't know a damn thing. Little Miss Goodie-Two-Shoes. You couldn't believe your precious Daddy could take me to a New Year's Eve Party and get us both drunk. One of the local cops drove behind us to make sure we made it home."

"But, Mother, you were both drunk. So, why was it all Daddy's fault?"

"You are right about the drunk part, but I had had enough. Not Matt. He followed me in my room laughing like when we first met, all glassy-eyed, threw me on the bed and tore my clothes off. When we were young, I thought that was love but by then I knew it was pure lust. I'll tell you this, after Izzie was born I never let him in my bedroom again."

Before I could slow her down, Izzie, her face red and sweaty, ran into the living room screaming.

"You rotten mother. How dare you discredit our father when he isn't here to tell his side of the story?"

"Don't you look at me like that." Olivia yelled at her. "You look just like Jessie did when I told him about his brother and what he did to me. Jessie had that same crazed look that you have now but he, at least, showed some compassion. Stop it. I couldn't care less about the lot of you."

Turning to Hannah, Olivia shrieked, "Why do you think I cared for you so much more than Izzie? I may have had to marry Matt because I was foolish enough to get pregnant, but I loved you. Then Izzie came along."

With that statement their conversation ended abruptly.

Izzie rubbed her hand over her forehead as she ran from the room toward the front door. Her sweaty hand grasped the brass door handle.

It opened. She stepped forward, tripped on the Persian rug and fell to the floor. I licked her face but could not help her, so I hurried through the open door to the nearest bush just in time to save the Persian rug. By the time I got back inside Hannah had called Jake.

What a day it had been. No wonder I had a restless night.

Chapter 16

Izzie seemed dazed and still on the floor when Jake came to Olivas's to carry us to his house. He had very little to say as he drove us back to the lodge. Hannah rushed to get in her car and followed us out the driveway. Olivia yelled one of her bad words as I hopped in the back seat. I looked out the back-car window and saw her waving her arms in the air like a bird unable to fly. Oh boy, that woman was a crazy one.

Last night ended in resentment and bitter sadness. We slept snuggled together for a restful sleep--me and Izzie, not me and Jake.

Knock, knock.

Not now, I thought. Go away. I was having a great dream. Oh, I was so close to getting the upper hand on that stinky barn cat with the big black and white tail.

Knock, knock.

Rats, I might as well jump off the bed and bark. Sometimes I bark a couple times to wake her. Izzie sat up, slowly stood up, and stepped toward the door. Too bad. I had forgotten to carry turtle to bed last night, left him on the floor. Too late. Izzie stumbled over him, grabbed the bedpost and fell back on the bed. Another typical day was beginning.

Izzie's bare feet scuffed on the wood floor as she headed toward the sound. The door squeaked as she opened it.

Jake came into the bedroom. "How about a tray of goodies and steaming hot coffee?"

I'm sure he brought coffee made with that French Press thing-a-ma-jig. Izzie was all smiles, did some stretches as Jake laid the breakfast goodies on a small table.

"You're the sweetest brother ever."

"You're the sweetest sister ever." His eyes had that mischievous glimmer they got when he teased Izzie. She told me they were the best of friends growing up although they didn't see a lot of each other. Olivia had made sure Jake was sent to Kemper Military Academy, so they only saw each other on summer vacations. His holidays were spent with his mother.

When he teased me, I needed to look way up, about two and half times higher than Buddy. Jake's body was muscular. Mommadog said he wrestled in college. He carried himself with shoulders and chest erect. His blue eyes were one of his distinctive features. They were like the water in my water bowl, sparkly and bright. A unique scar on his right jaw was partly hidden under a short-cropped black beard. His hair was like the poodle's who sometimes visits Daisy, short, black and curly.

Sometimes when he looked at Izzie, touched her hair or shoulder I thought he loved—oh, no, I guess it had been my imagination.

I took my morning downward dog to a new level by rolling over on my back and twisting for a full minute. A few final strong scratches to my head and I was ready for the day. Izzie showered and we headed downstairs to the kitchen. She settled into the breakfast nook while I ran through the doggie door. I hurried, took care of business and got back inside just in time to see Izzie pour herself some orange juice in a frosted glass from the freezer. She handed me one of the last four pieces of bacon on the breakfast plate.

"I set the table an hour ago, the bacon is probably cold," Jake said.

I licked my whiskers doubting if another piece would come my way because, at that very minute, Buddy ran around the corner so fast he slid into the table. Dishes, silverware, coffee, OJ, and my bacon slid to the floor. My so-called friend, Buddy, beat me to the bacon.

Jake grabbed paper towels, a wet sponge, and began to clean up the mess.

"Hannah called a couple of hours ago to ask if you were feeling better. She has a headache but was leaving to drive someplace with Patrick. I don't remember what else she said. Something about the police wanting Patrick to bring Guffin into the station to answer some questions. She was going with them."

"Why do they want to talk to Guffin? Couldn't they leave that poor man alone? He's been through so much and now they want to talk. This is ridiculous."

Ring. Ring. Jake answered the phone.

"Well, yes, Sheriff Henshaw. You found what? No problem, we'll finish breakfast and come over. I'm glad you called. No, I haven't heard from Father. No, really, I have no idea why his truck would be parked way out there."

He turned to Izzie. Those bright blue eyes had a curious stare as he hung up the phone.

"Father Sim's truck has been found abandoned beside Horn Lake about ten miles from town. The first quarter of his truck was on a sloping embankment partway into the lake. They're thinking this could be serious, a drowning or even suicide. Do you recall anything unusual in your conversation?"

"Nothing. Have they checked the rectory?"

"Yes, again this morning when they realized it was his truck. Let's finish and go out to the lake."

Go? Did I hear the word go? Buddy was too fast for me. He headed for the kitchen door, but I had the last laugh. He dropped a two-inch bite of crispy bacon and I grabbed it. We made it to the car just as Izzie opened the door of the jeep. We jumped in before her. Unfortunately, we pushed her causing her to drop her plastic thermos of coffee. The lid popped off, coffee everywhere. Another mess.

Jake took a last gulp of his coffee and went back in the house to fill another thermos for Izzie. The green paint on this old one was scratched and dented. Better for Izzie's than something new. A better lid, for sure. "Maybe we can be of some help. Let's go. Sheriff Henshaw said they are treating this as an abandoned vehicle and going to tow the truck to the county parking lot this afternoon."

We turned off the highway onto a narrow dirt road leading us through woods running to Lake Horn. Kudzu hung from giant oaks, which stood tall and straight holding the demanding vine. Others, at one time stately and imposing, lay fallen, with peeling bark that revealed their creamy skin. We drove through a dark tunnel. I wondered what we would find on the other side. I had that twisty turning in my tummy. It was not a good feeling. On this road, there was only one way in, and one way out. Several Sheriff and County cars were ahead of us, so the last few miles were thick with red dust.

Izzie opened the car door. Buddy and I jumped out and surveyed the scene. The truck was still parked as Sheriff Henshaw had described it, headed down a steep slope toward the water with the front bumper submerged in water.

"Was someone in a hurry? Why would a truck be on such a steep slope and part-way in the lake?" I woofed to Buddy. As you might expect, he didn't have a clue. While Buddy sniffed the tires, I put my nose to the ground checking for anything the tall humans couldn't see or smell. It still surprises me how much they miss up there.

Tire tracks showed the direction the truck was headed but they looked brushed over in a side to side manner. Someone had scattered some dried, musty leaves and sticks along the way.

Then, I caught a whiff. My nose twitched.

"Woof, woof," I said.

Buddy came running. I'd picked up on something odd. There was something peculiar in the way the dirt smelled. Maybe it was motor oil. This new smell was behind the truck, between the tires. It led up into the truck bed. The same smell was in the truck bed and on the ground.

Buddy and I growled. We tried short yaps. I was never a yapper, and neither was Buddy. This went on for a couple minutes until we got their attention. Izzie turned and hurried to me. She knows the way I sound when I find something.

"Sheriff, something's wrong. Both dogs are barking and sniffing the ground. Buddy's just jumped in the truck bed," Izzie said.

"Let's take a look. Come over here, Deputy. Do you smell anything?" The sheriff shifted from one foot to the other. "Get down on your knees, closer to the ground. Let's move these leaves and brush. Is that another track? Did it come down from the truck bed?"

"Well, I'll be damned, I think it did, Sir," the deputy said. "Looks like a motorcycle tire track to me."

"Okay, everyone back away. Deputy's Hunt and Logsdon, over here, secure the scene."

"Yes, Sir," Hunt answered.

"Deputy Logsdon come with me back to the scene of the fire. I think we may have more on our hands than an abandoned vehicle."

Chapter 17

From time to time I have what you humans call a gut feeling. At these moments my interest begins to grow, and I have a misgiving we're on the verge of something big. My big, brown sidekick was also paying close attention to the excitement as we bounced into the car to leave the lake.

Dark, thunderous clouds blanketed the car as we left the lake and began the drive toward the church, or to what had been the church.

With our noses barely stuck out the back window, rain sprinkled our muzzles. Izzie had a rule for Buddy and me to never put our heads out of the window, but noses were okay. It was still one of those hot muggy days that cried for a rain. That was another odd saying of Izzie's. We all knew a day could not cry, none of my days ever did. My days were all too happy to cause any crying.

Buddy and I bounced out of the car to hear the deep voice of the Fire Marshall talking to Sheriff Henshaw and Jake. The sheriff yanked up his jeans and spit some brown stuff on the ground. His suspenders did not accomplish their intended use.

"My fire investigators finally cleared a way to the left side of the basement with all the evidence showing this is where the fire started," the Marshall said. "We kinda thought the accelerant was somewheres in the storage area where they keep the cleaning supplies, rags an' the like or, maybe, in the kitchen, you know, a likely place with the gas stove an' all."

"But the stove hadn't been used for days. As far as I know, it hasn't been used since the funeral dinner," said Jake.

"You're right. The massive destruction on that side of the basement made us think at first someone was cooking," the Fire Marshall answered. "Get this, to my surprise that thar accelerant was gasoline."

"Gasoline? Then you must think it is arson." Piped in spit-man sheriff.

"Rightly so. There was an empty gas can next to the generator kept for when the power goes out."

"Hey, Marshall," shouted one of the firemen from the basement. "You'd better get down here ASAP and have a look."

"What is it?"

"That storage room behind the kitchen, the one that's part way behind the freezer, well, Sir, there's sure enough a burned body in there."

"What are you talking about, a person or an animal?" The Marshall yelled as he raced down the stairs motioning all but Sheriff Henshaw to stay behind. Henshaw yanked up his jeans, spit, and followed.

I turned to Buddy and woofed, "I'd told you a few days ago I didn't like the smell from inside this church."

Buddy made eye contact with me, then dashed down the basement stairway. Not to be outdone by a lab, I followed about two feet behind. He beat me to the bottom, but I was close enough to bump into him when he swerved to miss a hand that reached for his collar. That maneuver allowed me to wiggle under the stairs. A good place to hide.

"Dammed dogs. Get them out of here," yelled the Sheriff to one of his guys.

But not before I picked up a scent from under the stairs. Something I knew, something I recognized. Just couldn't put my nose to it. What was this familiar smell? Where was it coming from? Against the dark wall under the stairway, I dug through the clutter of newspapers until, there it was, a hammer. That particular hammer smell held a memory. What was so obvious?

"Buddy, you smell anything familiar down here?" I woofed.

"Of course, smoke, whaddya' think I smell. Didn't ya know things had been burning down here?" he woofed back.

"Naw, this is something different. Have we seen this hammer before? No answer from Buddy. I was suddenly real, real hungry. Maybe I needed some chow. Steak tips would be nice or maybe some barbeque. Then I remembered, barbeque.

Chapter 18

Buddy and I ran up the basement steps as fast as we could go with the Fire Marshall waving his arms close behind. The mood was somber as Jake drove us all home. Maybe because Buddy and I got into trouble or maybe because of the investigation. I wasn't sure. Four of us, two with two legs and two with four legs trudged into Jake's kitchen just as the phone rang.

"Glad you called. You've left the police station? Taken Guffin home? Okay, come on over and we'll catch up while I cook some steaks." Jake hung up the phone.

"Was that Patrick?"

"Yes, we agreed we all need a relaxing visit. They'll be over soon for a steak and plenty of talk. I'll open us a beer and light the grill.

"I'll wash up and start a salad."

Izzie's arms were full as she gathered romaine, carrots, radishes, and a cucumber from the stainless-steel refrigerator. She placed the final produce on top. A red ripe tomato immediately slid from her hand and fell to the floor. Naturally, she stepped on it. Squished seeds and red plump tomato flesh sprayed everywhere. Not to worry, Buddy and I loved tomatoes, so we hurriedly licked up her mess. We'd done a good job by the time she got to the roll of paper towels.

"That darn thing rolled right out of my hand."

My gal needed watching. There was a comment I'd heard people make—she's all thumbs. Let me tell you my Momma was a sweet lady and there was a lot more to Izzie than thumbs. I remember, Grandog said she's been a klutz since childhood. I doubt I can expect any change as she ages.

Talk from the deck outside let us know Hannah and Patrick were here. Buddy galumphed out to meet them with me coming up about six dog steps behind. Both people could be counted on for some really good ear scratching.

Cold beer was passed while Buddy and I went to the pool for our drop and fetch game. The party moved outside to talk while Jake watched over his steaks. We stayed close enough to hear about the questioning Griffin and Patrick endured at the police station.

"It was pretty upsetting," said Patrick. "Grandad broke down and confessed he had lied about the night he found Grandmother. He hadn't driven a load of cattle to market but had been on an all-night crap shoot with his pals."

"I bet that was news to the detective," said Jake.

"No, most people around here know my folks have had words about this." Patrick frowned. "Grandad was so used to lying to her that he just blurted out about the cattle without thinking. It did not go well today, but none of us think he would ever hurt her. They released him but warned him to stay close and not leave Nesbit. He's exhausted so we took him straight home and Hannah opened him some navy bean soup. Good old Campbell's."

"Do you think they believed him?" asked Izzie.

"They seemed to, but who knows what those guys are thinking. It's the norm to look to the family members first and check their alibies. They've been easy on me. They know I was in Nashville, so my questioning was way smoother than Grandad's. We all loved grandmother Clarabelle so much. This is a nuisance. Their questioning will, I pray, stop soon. Now with the body in the church, they have their hands full and may relax on grandad a bit. Has anyone said who or what it was they found?"

"Not a clue. They ran us out of there after the dog episode," said Izzie.

"What do you mean?" Hannah's hands rested on her hips. "Dog episode?"

"Oh, yes, our two super sleuths decided to go in the basement for whatever reason. Sheriff Henshaw did not take kindly to their interference and chased them out. We all made a hasty retreat at that point."

Hannah laughed and patted her lap for me to jump up. A sense of humor like Hannah's changed the mood instantly. A good ear scratch followed. Hannah sipped her beer and winked at me. She was like my second mother.

"I'll give these steaks and potatoes a turn and they're ready. You gals can go in and get the salad from the fridge," Jake said. "Don't need to feed the dogs. I've grilled some liver for our four-legged friends."

We ran close behind Jake when he placed the food on the picnic table. Our usual place underneath the seats allowed for tidbits to come our way. Conversation from above proved informative as we shared bites of liver jerky.

They continued the conversation about the dead something in the church basement. Buddy and I knew from the smell that it was a person. Dogs are smart in a lot of ways. I am proud to say I inherited a nose for such things.

"Hey, Izzie, I nearly forgot. As soon as you finish your ice cream, let's go out to the car. Guffin sent you a present," Patrick said.

"A present?"

"Yes, he said he remembered you saying to Clarabelle that you thought her ironing board would make you a great coffee table. He wants you to have it. He's for sure he will never do any ironing."

"Oh, that's so sweet of him. Yes, I'd love to have it. I can tell from the underside, it's really pretty wood or would be if I sanded it down."

"I'm just curious, who turns an ironing board into a coffee table?" asked Patrick.

"I will. The look is called 'Shabby Chic'. It's a decorating style where furniture and furnishings are either chosen for their appearance of age and signs of wear and tear or the item is refurbished to look worn."

"People actually spend money on old worn stuff?" Patrick shook his head in bewilderment and disapproval.

"Some people even take new items, paint them and distress them to achieve the appearance of an antique. It's the soft relaxed style that I use in the loft. A lot of cabbage roses and ivy, you know, homey stuff."

"Okay. Whatever you say. Well, Jake, let's go unload that 'shabby' ironing board so Izzie can get started making it into something 'chic'."

"Maybe we should just stick to shabby," Jake answered.

I turned to Buddy. "Here we go again. Who ever heard of a cabbage rose? I, myself, hate the taste of cabbage and would not be caught dead tasting a cabbage and a rose together. Some of these humans sure do have weird tastes."

The phone rang. Jake raced into the kitchen to answer. I followed him and stood beside the screen door to listen. "Sure, Mom, I can come to Caruthersville tomorrow. About three o'clock will work for me. Supper, sure thing."

"Is Janet okay?" Izzie asked when Jake returned.

"Yes, she wants to talk to me about some decisions she's made."

I reminded Buddy that Olivia was Jake's stepmother and Janet was Jake's real mother. Janet and Jake were very close. I wondered why she wanted to see him.

Chapter 19

It was so humid in Mississippi my eyes were sweating as Izzie and I drove to Memphis with her 'shabby' ironing board in the back seat. It was no cooler as we headed into Tennessee but riding in the comfort of air conditioning made me much more comfortable.

Izzie glanced over the back seat to talk to me. "Who do you think they found in that basement fire? Do you think it might be Father Sims?"

How should I know? I was doing my best to keep the facts straight. I decided it best to not growl. The smoky damp smell of the burned-out basement was not easy to forget, but neither was the smell of burned flesh. I wondered if Izzie smelled it. Not knowing for sure who was down there became very puzzling. My nose would become one of my greatest assets, I'd soon learn.

Wasn't Father Sims still missing? That was a matter for my deepest thinking, like the time I caught the possums eating the dog food in Jake's basement. Well, not exactly the same, but that investigation also took some deep thinking. Buddy and I finally caught the rascals by hiding in that dark, damp basement until the sun came up. Maybe we needed to hide now, that is if we could get away from the angry Fire Marshall.

So much happened in the two weeks since Clarabelle's death. That situation caused me to pause. We'd made the last stoplight before home when I came out of my daze and put my brain into second gear.

Izzie pulled into the underground garage. "I'll set up the ironing board, take a thirty-minute nap, then work my twelve-hour shift tonight at seven o'clock. Jake is spending the day and tonight with his mom in Caruthersville, then he's coming through Memphis on his way home to Nesbit tomorrow."

Great. Buddy and I needed to work on a strategy like Perry Mason would do. When we got back to Nesbit, we needed to have a plan to know exactly how to get into the church basement.

No sooner had we settled into our nap than it was over. I was awakened as Izzie walked toward the front door.

"I bet Jake would like some relaxing time on the boat. I'll stop at Kroger and get some chicken to grill. I guess you want me to grill you doggies some more beef liver. Be back in a while."

Yum, yum. Saliva dripped off my tongue. My sweet momma really loved me.

Chapter 20

Before Izzie left for work, she turned on my Perry Mason reruns. I watched his reruns a lot, Perry and I solved several crimes together.

Izzie said she'd be home a little after seven. She used the time words a lot. No matter how hard I stared, I couldn't read the clock in the hall. The sun was up, so I could count on her to bounce in the door at any time.

Crash. Thud.

"Darn it."

My sweet momma was home. I ran to the hall to get a hug. Opps. She tripped on a white untied shoelace and fell against the loveseat inside the doorway. Groceries went everywhere. My Sweetie needed to investigate a purchase of nurse shoes that hook with that sticky stuff like what's on my winter coat.

With one arm holding the ripped Kroger sack, Izzie used the other to give my head a loving pat.

Izzie could leave St Jude's and be here at the loft in fifteen minutes on a bad traffic day. With little traffic that Thursday morning, she probably made the trip even faster.

"Come on, Sammy. Let's go to the courtyard. Are you ready to explode, Little Love Sponge?"

I finished my business after three good sniffs by the magnolia tree and two at the faded red azalea bushes. Sabbath, the Doberman, must have eaten some asparagus from the smell of things.

"Let's go back inside, Sammy. We need a nap."

Poor, forgetful Izzie, didn't she remember I slept while she was at work. When I smelled Daisy out in the hall I did revive myself to give her some loud barks, just friendly ones. I had more sniffing to do in the courtyard, but I could tell by Izzie's voice she was not fooling. She wanted to get her nap. I followed her like a good-natured doggie.

The afternoon sun was beginning to peek through the sunshades when Izzie stirred from her nap. She stretched, yawned, and bounced up ready to get busy. The AC blew constantly which told me it must be miserable outside.

With our nap over, Izzie fixed herself a protein powder, spinach, kale, and strawberry smoothie and gave me a boiled egg. She called this drink her energy booster, but it did nothing for me. One time, well, more than once, she'd spilled some on the floor. I tried it and I can tell you it's not a good thing for dogs to drink. For you humans, perhaps the jury is still out.

Izzie clutched her smoothie in one hand while she measured the ironing board. She went to the storage closet and brought in a large, blue tarp. The only place large enough to spread out the tarp to catch the mess she'd probably make was the end of the kitchen next to the living room. The rough surface of the tarp was a good back scratcher, so I rolled around on it paying particular attention to that hard-to-reach itchy spot between my shoulder blades.

"Clarabelle must have three different covers on this board to make it soft. This is a mess." Izzie took a hammer and screwdriver and tried to pry out the staples which held down the first cover.

Bad idea. No sooner had she picked up the hammer then it mysteriously left her hand and landed on her right big toe. Momma is so talented. She can really hop. Poor Momma. She hopped into the kitchen, opened the freezer and found a frozen bag of peas to put on her toe. So much for getting those nails out of the ironing board.

"Maybe Jake will help me pull out these darn nails or staples or whatever they are," Izzie sighed as she rubbed her aching toe. "Look, Sammy, my toe is turning blue." She hopped to her sectional by the wall of windows. I jumped up beside her.

The building we lived in was an old converted warehouse. Our loft had three old brick walls and one glass wall. The glass wall let me look for miles at the Mississippi River and the City of Memphis. Sometimes at night I sat and gazed through the glass to see the twinkling lights of boats on the river. My fluffy tail wagged. Tap. Tap. Tap. The rhythm of my wagging made me feel at peace. I had that same tranquil feeling sitting with Izzie that night.

Many nights when Izzie drove into the garage I felt the same calm, no worries. No one could park under there unless they had a button to press which opened an iron gate. People could also come in through the massive wooden front doors off the courtyard. The courtyard was one of my very favorite places in the whole wide world. After my visit to the courtyard we went up to the loft.

We used what was called a freight elevator to get to the fourth floor. Two apartments, mine and Daisy's, occupied this fourth level. I had never thought of Izzie and myself as freight, but who knows in this crazy world.

Izzie was still rubbing her toe when I heard a thud. The freight elevator had arrived and so had my pal, Buddy. I jumped off the sectional and scampered toward the hallway. Jake was a close second as Buddy bounced through the door and began slurping from my water bowl. He was so sloppy one would have thought he was related to Izzie.

I got a scratch on my right ear from Jake as he came through the door. He picked my sweet momma off the floor like a rag doll and gave her a swirling hug. Of course, the bag of frozen peas fell off her toe and dropped directly on my head. Man, that was the coolest I'd been all day.

Jake wanted to talk, something about his mother's letter, but Izzie had food packed and hurried us down the freight elevator, into her car. I got a whiff of the river as we turned on to Riverside Drive. It was a short drive to the Mud Island Marina where Izzie's boat was docked.

My paws sweated from the heat as I ran toward the boat. It was cooler on the boat 'cause Old Man River had a nice breeze blowing. Izzie washed and filled our water bowls as Jake handed Izzie a cold drink from the cooler. He got one for himself and plopped down on the leather sofa.

"Izzie, you won't believe what Mom wanted to talk about. She's getting married to Rocco."

"She's doing what?"

"She wanted my blessing. Of course, I've known Rocco since I was a kid. I remember summers working for Dad and Rocco in their construction company. Dad always gave Rocco credit for believing in him when Dad was a teenager. He's always been around, especially after Dad died, even helped me with college tuition. I just never thought of them together, like married."

"Think about it." Izzie wiped water drops from the beer can on her jeans. "He's a handsome man with his snow-white beard and your mother is so pretty they would make a striking couple. You know, sometimes love is blind, then all of a sudden it hits you. Remember, they've known each other for a long time. It was Rocco that got Dad and Janice to move to Memphis. Maybe when Rocco's wife died last year it just seemed natural they'd get together.

"By the way, have you talked to your mom or sister since your mother's outburst?"

"No. I haven't, and I don't care if I ever speak or hear from Olivia ever."

"I agree she really showed herself that night." Jake stood to get another beer. "However, as you grew up you've had some good memories."

"Not many," Izzie countered.

"What I mean is, she was drinking. You know she exaggerates after drinking too much alcohol."

"She embellished everything. I know she lied about Daddy." Izzie's chin stuck out. "He's not here to defend himself. After all these years, I still miss him. She had no right to dishonor him like she did."

"Hey, I didn't mean to interfere," Jake leaned over and patted my sweetie's arm. "Back to my mom, I have no problem with her being happy, but there's a lot more to it. She gave me this envelope for us to read. I wasn't to open it until..."

Another boat came along side with greetings yelled from the occupants. The conversation ended.

"Come on board for a cold beer or some sweet tea," Izzie yelled.

Quickly the cruiser was full of people, probably ten or so according to Buddy who was better at counting than me. We ran for the master suite where we could jump on the bed and have a rest. Once we dug back the shiny bedspread we snuggled against the pillows for a nap. Buddy was snoring as I drifted off, remembering another cocktail party when I was a young puppy.

Chapter 21

I'd had this dream before, remembering Momma loved to have parties. She could have a party for any occasion, some I had never heard of: The First Day of Spring Party, Arbor Day Party, St. Patrick's Day Party, and of course, a Happy New Year's Eve Party. When events evaded her, there was always the old stand-by—The Cocktail party.

Sometimes I thought she planned parties so she could clean even more than the waxing, mopping, and dusting that took place every Saturday morning. This was the way Clarabelle taught her to clean, and I can assure you old habits do not die easily. Clarabelle could see dust in the sunlight coming through the windowpane. I swear she would hold the handle of the Electrolux in midair to catch the dust particles.

Sometimes I tracked in a lot of dirt and was reminded of it. I knew I had misbehaved by the firmness of Momma's voice when she sent me to the living room corner.

Any punishment was well worth the prize. Izzie never realized as she heaped piles of little sandwiches on the coffee table, I was within snatching distance. I remember she placed food everywhere except the bathrooms.

On party day, I had a relaxing, good smelly bath. My grey and black flowing curls were washed and brushed until silky, then momma decked me out with a neck scarf or fancy collar. I admit I was a bit of a showoff. Remember, I was the only youngster in the household and so it was what it was.

I looked good. I smelled good. I was ready for the party to begin.

Everything was in readiness. Glasses, both highball and martini, shiny without one water spot, had been placed on the bar between the kitchen and living room. This lay-out was handy for those needing light or heavy refreshment which, as I remember, they all needed.

Clear, round, glass cocktail plates with gold embossed flowers rimming the edges added a festive appearance to her much-labored food items. The dining room table welcomed friends to an assortment of cheeses and tiny meat balls, which were my favorite. I hated the barbeque sauce they were hiding in. Guests always liked the little roll-up tidbits of meat around a tiny sweet pickle. The pickle could be left out if I had made them. Of course, I never helped. No one was allowed in the kitchen as Momma and Clarabelle prepared their party dishes.

I was always eager for Momma's parties to start. My eyes were wide with excitement as I greeted her guests at the front door. I barked a pleasant greeting which welcomed each guest. Handshakes and pats were shared by friends old and new, then on to the bar for food and drink. By this time, I was usually shut out of the conversation. Granted I had little to offer but that did not diminish my desire to be at the center of it all.

In my dream I distinctively remembered the ladies' conversation turned to antique quilts of which Olivia had several. A double wedding ring in shades of yellow with a tiny, blue, flower print was a showstopper. One of my favorites was Izzie's when she was little. It was a bright blue and white quilt with ten little Dutch Girls made by Izzie's Grandmother. Of all the quilts, my absolutely most favorite to look at was the red poppy quilt. Nothing but shades of red poppies with green stems laced each flower on a stark white background. It hung on the wall behind the dollies who sat quietly in their little rockers.

The discussion turned to patterns, hand stitching, and colors. Momma offered to show the ladies some of her collections in the back bedroom.

With wine glasses in hand, six or seven ladies followed her down the long hall. Entering the room, they observed quilts hanging on three walls and draped over anything that wasn't moving. The ladies stood in a semi-circle. They were shown various objects made from quilts including a couple of dollies with red and blue calico quilted dresses.

I had been left behind in the living room. No one asked me to follow. This left me at a loss for how I could be recognized. Earlier I hid a treasure between the sofa cushions, but no one had discovered it. I needed to take more drastic steps. Out of the blue, it came to me. The ladies Momma tried to impress needed to have a special memory from this party. I ran down the hallway as fast as my short legs could carry me.

I pushed through the women who had crowded together. With a feeling of mischief, I opened my mouth and grabbed the loveliest dolly in the room. I gently drug her to the center of the room. With all the energy any six-month Shih Tzu puppy could muster I began to hump Momma's dolly.

One lady, wearing black satin jeans, laughed. "Thank goodness he doesn't like pant legs."

Izzie had a tight-lipped smile as she did her best to hide her embarrassment by laughing with the ladies. She went back to the living room and showed her unhappiness by shaking her finger at me. She turned toward the bar, then spotted one of the guests holding up a greasy steak bone he'd retrieved from between the sofa cushions. I hung my head, starring at the floor. My sweet momma growled just like Mommadog.

My dream ended. Buddy and I heard Jake call us. It was fun to rest as I recalled my puppy actions at one of momma's cocktail parties.

"Wake up guys. Get off that bed before Izzie sees you or you'll be in trouble with the boss. Time to close down the boat and go home."

The moon was high when we left the cruiser. I still love dollies.

Chapter 22

Before our nap that night, Buddy had been his normal friendly self. He gently laid his head on the knee of any willing guest. I admit his big brown eyes express a kindness everyone liked. He was so big, yet so shy, the ladies wanted to give him some of my hugs.

I am confident in my approach to Izzie's friends. She said my problem was I shake with my left paw. It always got me a shake plus a scratch on my right ear, so I'd say, it worked for me. Another great trick was when I rolled over and played dead as Izzie pointed her finger at me and said "Bang, Bang". My reward was applause and sometimes a treat.

That next morning was another matter. Breakfast for Izzie and Jake started with the French press coffee while Buddy and I waited close to the stove in case Izzie dropped a sausage link. As she placed the scrambled eggs on the platter, it happened. Two sausages rolled off. Oh, this was starting to be a good day and I hadn't been to my courtyard yet.

"Jake, yesterday, I tried to remove those scorched covers from

Clarabelle's ironing board and couldn't get the first one off. Could you help me?"

"Sure, just let me pour another cup of coffee. Where're your tools?"

"On the floor, at the end under the counter."

"Okay, let's get this done. I need to tell you more about Mother and Rocco."

"Can you wait a few minutes? The boys need to go to the courtyard. It shouldn't take them long. Be back in a jiffy." She grabbed our leashes and we were out the door. I jumped in the elevator. Buddy was close behind. We wasted no time with our important morning business.

Daisy rode up with us as Momma talked to Mr. Cohen. They usually chattered about the weather as Mr. Cohen tugged at his suspenders. Seemed without purpose to me. I believed conversation about the weather was the mannerly way humans were friendly. I preferred sniffing.

Buddy and I ran to our water bowl. Again, he splashed water on the floor.

Jake had a screwdriver in one hand and a tack hammer in the other, busy prying out the nails from the ironing board.

"When they marry, Mom's moving into Rocco's home. Can you believe she wants me to have a room there? I asked her why a man my age would want a room with her and Rocco. Seems silly to me."

"Maybe she wanted to make you feel welcome and at home when you visit them. He has no family, no children."

"Perhaps you're right. As soon as I finish this we need to read the letter she gave me. Wow, Clarabelle sure meant business when she hammered in these staples. She wanted to make sure this ironing board was completely covered. These staples are in to stay. Hand me the wider screwdriver, please."

Long ago Clarabelle said to me her ironing board was her safety net. Maybe Jake would figure out what she meant when he finished.

Jake sighed as he pulled out the staples from the third and final cover. The phone rang. Izzie answered.

“Are you sure? Dental charts. Really? No, I know of no next-of-kin. He had no siblings and his parents died years ago in a car wreck,” Izzie said. “Okay. Jake’s here. Yes, we can come in today if that’s what you want.”

Izzie hung up the phone and turned slowly toward Jake shaking her head. Her hands covered her mouth. She stared at us with wide eyes as she backed onto the sectional.

“That was Sheriff Henshaw. They’ve taken the body from the church to the morgue. All indications are that it’s Father Sims. The sheriff wants to go over the last few days with us if we can come in today.”

“Father Sims.” Jake ran his hands through his hair. “Are they sure? Not him? This is too much. Aren’t you scheduled to work tonight?”

“They’re pretty sure. Oh, no. I mean, yes, I can go. I don’t go in for three days. This is unbelievable.”

“I’ll go on down. Can you and Sammy leave soon? We can meet at my house, then go together. Here, I loosened the rest of the staples. Do you want me to finish this? I can get this last cover off if you want.”

“No, let’s just leave this mess. I can finish the last cover when I get back. I’ll grab some things, put Sammy’s food in the car and be on the road in about thirty.”

Looked like Buddy and I could get to work solving the case sooner than I’d expected. I explained the plan about getting into the church. Buddy agreed everyone would be too busy to pay any attention to where we were or what we were doing. We each grabbed a super chewy bone from my hiding place. Buddy followed Jake giving me a sideways glance as he sprinted through the door toward the freight elevator.

I forgot to tell Buddy I'd hidden the hammer under the church steps. The cops and firemen were too busy to look through a pile of newspapers under the steps. Buddy and I would find it when we got back to the church. Come on Izzie, time's wasting. I got one last cool drink as Momma opened the door to leave.

"Clarabelle and now Father Sims," Izzie said to me as I hoofed it into the elevator. "Sammy, could there be a connection? The unexplained deaths of two such pious people seem like an odd coincidence to me, don't you agree?"

Izzie opened the back-car door and I jumped inside. Did she really expect me to answer? I thought it better to cock my head and whine a little. Izzie blew me a kiss in the back seat. We drove toward Nesbit, Mississippi at ticket-risking speed. Our lines of communication could greatly improve. She needed to learn dogspeak.

Chapter 23

Our tires crunched in the gravel as we neared Jake's lodge. The scent of the honeysuckle was strong as I jumped from the back seat to the driveway. Izzie relaxed a bit in Jake's quick embrace, then they were off.

Jake said we were to stay home because they were going to the morgue. Buddy and I were left in the yard to play. Izzie and Jake had no clue we were on our own search mission. As soon as Jake and Izzie drove around the circle drive in front, Buddy and I ran through the back-soybean field toward the church. We covered the mile in good form.

Constantly alert, we slowly crept through the parking lot toward the front of the church. The Fire Marshall was nowhere to be seen, so we scurried through the open doorway amid ash and fallen plaster and made our way toward the basement steps.

A strange sound caused Buddy to stop so abruptly I ran right into his bottom. That was nothing you want to do very often. He was so tall my head went between his hind legs. We both had stopped. Something was rustling through the papers in the basement where I'd hid the hammer.

Slowly we descended the steps. Something scurried across the floor. Halfway down I spied the hideous monster.

"Oh my, Buddy," I growled. "That was a possum, probably looking for something to eat." Buddy took charge and let out a fierce bark that must have scared the intruder because the poor critter ran to the other side of the basement. What a pal, my Buddy.

We sniffed around the basement and found where gasoline had been poured. Smoke-covered appliances clued us the fire started close by. A charred wall and hole in the ceiling suggested this was what Perry would call the point of ignition. My sensitive smeller told me this was not an enormous fire. Something else had been the cause of death here. I took a final sniff, then trotted to the far side of the basement where the hammer was hidden.

Buddy followed me to the area under the steps. The space was dark and smelled musty despite the fire. Sure enough, under trash and newspapers, I found the hammer. Buddy jumped at it, but I barked to hold him off. He needed to get a good smell. I hoped he'd come to my same conclusion.

"What do ya think?" I barked. The smell of barbeque still lingered. There was something else, the odor of someone I knew. The guys in the band used Guffin's tools to build the stage so we could smell Guffin, but there was also another strong smell. Another person we knew.

"Wait," I growled. "That's the smell of Uncle Jessie."

"Yup," Buddy woofed. "Jessie worked on the stage too. So, what was a tool like this doing down here in the basement where someone had just died?"

"Think about it, Buddy," I barked. "We've found the murder weapon."

At that moment we heard talking from the vestibule above. Buddy's teeth grabbed the wooden handle of the hammer. We ran up the steps. We moved fast, as fast as any super sniffing dogs could travel. Two steps from the top Buddy tripped, caught himself and kept running but, in the process he dropped the hammer. It slid through the steps and landed with a thud on the trash below.

"What are you dogs doing here?" yelled one of the male voices.

I thought it best not to answer. We scampered past him so fast Buddy bumped his leg. He fell backward onto a heap of burned wood and plaster. Once we got out of the church we ran toward home. That voice yelled the same kind of words Mother Olivia used when she had been drinking. I don't think that man was drinking on the job. I wonder why he was so mad at us. He should have realized we were doing our best to help Izzie solve a crime.

"Where have you two been?" said Izzie as she got out of Jake's Jeep." "We left you playing in the yard. You both look terribly dirty for a little play day outside. Sammy, you need a bath. I'm really upset with you. I've more on my mind than bathing a dirty dog." Izzie frowned. "Get in the garage, I need to give you a good scrubbing."

Normally, bath day was a happy occasion, however, I went quietly without any woofs. She was right. I was a mess. I hated to be dirty.

Wow, what a day. I was finally clean and dry with a blue scarf around my neck. I looked quite stylish. Buddy got his bath from the garden hose. I needed a nap. Maybe I needed to do some crucial thinking. Buddy was in the sunroom with his head on his paws. He snored as I curled against him. My eyelids were heavy. What crime was I solving? Man, Buddy was a loud snorer.

Chapter 24

The smell of grilled asparagus brought me out of a deep sleep. My nose twitched. My tummy growled. I hoped some of that asparagus was for me. I approached Izzie and rubbed against her tanned leg.

A tidbit came toward me. I knew all was forgiven now that I was clean and smelled sweet. I got a whiff of grilled pimento cheese sandwiches. If that was on the lunch menu, I'd leave it for Buddy. He'd eat anything.

Izzie walked toward the kitchen sink, humming a tune as she sliced into a ripe tomato. "This beefsteak I picked from your garden this morning is delicious. Opps, I dropped a slice."

Why do humans get names mixed up by calling two very different things by the same name? Since my young days playing with the yacht club people, I considered myself an authority on beef steak. Never have I compared a good juicy T-bone to a tomato. Don't take me wrong, I can chomp down on a ripe tomato as good as anyone, man or beast. Why, I'd been known to swipe several off the bush before picking. This language mix-up is tiresome. A tomato was not steak. I wish you humans would make up your mind what you're going to call this round, red, juicy thing Izzie was slicing.

"Oh, man, will you give me a break. Enough, enough," I groaned.

Pulp, juice and tiny seeds slide on the floor within reach of my black nose. I smelled. It was a tomato. I ate every ripe morsel anyway.

"This is great pimento salad on sourdough bread," said Jake. "Hannah must have brought sandwiches this morning when we were with the Sheriff. It was in the fridge when we got home. What do you make of our conversation with Sheriff Henshaw?

"Based on the findings it looks like it was Father Sim's body they found in the fire," said Izzie. "Interesting. We were told Father was found face down with a blow to the back of head and more to the back of the body. Sheriff Henshaw called it rage killing. Father was an easy-going person. I cannot imagine who would want to hurt, much less kill him in such a heartless manner, do you?"

"Not a clue." Jake poured some sweet tea. "There is still no answer about what his truck was doing on that bluff heading into the lake. No wonder the Sheriff thought he had drowned or been swept downstream. Let's go on a drive out there after lunch and have a look around." Jake finished his last bit of pimento sandwich, asparagus, and beefsteak.

Go?

Buddy and I heard the magic word at the same time and jumped, ready to pounce toward whatever vehicle was the one of choice for the GO. We were always on alert for that word. We happily followed Jake and Izzie when they climbed into the Jeep for a GO to the lake.

We arrived at the lake to find Father Sim's blue truck still partially in the water with the bed resting on a ridge. The tailgate was raised, too high for Buddy to jump in. Buddy barked until Jake let it down. Buddy jumped in. I put my paws on the edge of the tailgate and looked into the truck bed. My feelings were hurt because I couldn't jump as high.

Buddy was busy digging through piles of smelly old rags and junk. What Buddy found was surprising. Jake took one look and announced he had better turn it in to the sheriff.

Buddy jumped out of the truck with the object in his mouth. He hit the dirty ground and dropped the weathered leather pouch. The strap popped open. Pieces of white paper covered with little black dots and lines fell out of the pouch. Something like a white rag was stuffed inside. The whole thing landed in the leaves and broken branches.

Jake twisted his mouth and frowned as he stared at the mess of papers on the dirt.

Tracks from the bed of the truck led toward the road through the brush. Everything was like we'd left it. The single track of a motorcycle. The attempt to cover it with leaves and twigs was in vain. Buddy dug them aside to reveal clear muddy tracks.

Chapter 25

We pulled into Jake's driveway. A suffocating mist hung in the air, typical of a July afternoon in Mississippi. The sun, starting to set behind the old magnolia tree, was barely reflected through a dull haze. Buddy and I ran straight to our water bowls for a cool drink. As always, Buddy splashed water all over the floor. My paws got wet standing there, but I didn't complain, Buddy had been a big help to me at the lake. It paid for us short dogs to have friends with long legs.

Jake was opening the fridge when the phone rang.

"Hello. Here, Izzie, it's for you."

"Hello, Hannah? What? When? So, what happened? Okay, we'll come over."

Izzie turned to Jake. "Mother Olivia fell down the hall staircase, well, halfway down and landed on her left shoulder. A strap on her sandal broke and she couldn't catch herself. Uncle Jessie was there, they were going out for dinner. He called the ambulance, then Hannah. Anyway, Hannah was at Patrick's, she got to Olivia's just as the paramedics arrived. They don't think anything is broken but they still want to take her in for observation."

"Do you need to change before you go? I'll feed the dogs, then drive you. Here, boys, come and get your supper, remember the doggie door's for you."

"Jake, I don't want to go to the hospital. How can I put myself through seeing her after her latest tantrum? She hates me. She resents that I was even born. Why should I put myself through the misery of seeing her right now?"

"I'll tell you why. She's still your Mother. Within her black heart there is still love for you. Your mother has two obsessions, Mah Jongg and liquor. That night it was the booze. She got carried away. This is characteristic of her after too much to drink. Come on, little one, I'll be with you for support. The guys have been fed. Let's go. We still need to get some time to read Mom's letter."

Jake hugged her tightly, then opened the back door for them to leave. A whiff of the hot damp air told me a downpour was about to hit. I felt the weather may be foretelling the trouble Izzie was headed into. The situation could put Izzie in her dark place but, maybe, with Jake with her, it could be avoided. Our earlier trip to the lake caused me to deep think. Buddy and I must review what we learned at the lake-front this afternoon.

It had been a long day, with no nap. Now that we were home I was doing some deep thinking, perhaps the answer to what happened to the good priest would come to me. First, sleep called, I curled up next to Buddy and had a snooze.

Did I dream? My sensations seemed real as I rolled and swished in the horse poop. Perhaps I was wrong. I didn't smell like horse manure and Izzie wasn't giving me a bath. I tried to snuggle against Buddy, but, hearing the back door open, he was off like the wind, leaving me to figure where I was and what was real.

I watched Jake and Izzie as they removed their raincoats and hung them on the green coat rack by the back door.

Jake gently massaged Izzie's shoulder blades. "That wasn't too bad an experience, was it?"

"Of course not, Jake." Izzie smiled at him as she adjusted her ponytail. "Mother was out like a light and didn't realize I was there until we were leaving," Izzie continued. "Wonder what she'll be like tomorrow when Hannah and Patrick bring her home?"

Chapter 26

The sun, shining through the window, shone directly into my eyes. Those darn mockingbirds were singing their hearts out. I considered crawling under the blanket, then thought better of the idea. Izzie was showering. I could smell the lemongrass soap she used. That smell made me feel great, like I was running wild through a field of yellow wildflowers.

I followed my routine of the downward dog, a forward stretch, and a neck turn, then flew down the stairs and bumped head-first into Buddy. We both had the same idea and there's only one doggie door, guess who made it first? There are some advantages to being small. You can squeeze through places before the big guys get close. Whee. Relief on the azaleas. I went back inside through the doggie door.

The oatmeal Jake was stirring made my nose twitch. Maybe I smelled cinnamon. Wait, maybe it was the sausage 'cause my nose is usually not a cinnamon twitcher.

"Hannah called while I was showering." Izzie walked into the kitchen, towel drying her hair. "Olivia's not being released today. Her shoulder fracture needed to be reset. Hannah agreed with me, I might as well go back to Memphis. As you remember, I left the loft in pretty much of a mess. I'll get things cleaned, work a shift and be ready to come back in a couple days if Hannah, or you, need me."

"I always need you, don't you know that?" Jake made eye contact as he touched her arm. "I still need to talk to you about Mom's wedding plans and the letter she gave me."

"She's not getting married for three months. Can't it wait? I really need to get Sammy loaded and on the road."

"Sure, finish your breakfast, then be on your way. I've got cattle fences to mend today."

Buddy and I got our morning Dasuquin, a good tasting soft chew that is a doggie joint supplement. As I've reached my senior years I take several supplements. Nearly as many as Izzie. She mixes these powders on my food, for my eyes, my heart, and a probiotic. She says that's why I'm so perky. I, of course, know it's my good family genes. I had barely finished the chew when Izzie was ready to drive back to Memphis. It was a quiet drive. We had lots to think about. I, more than Izzie, 'cause at that time she had no idea of my suspicions.

We arrived home. I raced full speed from the garage to the courtyard where Sabbath was busy digging behind the old magnolia. Dirt flew over his head. He was burying a bone the size of a whole ham. I decided against bothering him as he can get territorial when it comes to his bones. That red Doberman is way too big for me to argue with. Besides, I needed to get up to the loft and start my thinking.

The ride up the freight elevator was uneventful. We settled in the loft, I found my turtle and ball. Izzie found her broom and dustpan. She gave the broom a few half-hearted swipes across the floor, then stopped and laid the broom aside. Sweet momma walked to the ironing board and unwrapped the last covering from around her soon-to-be-table. Jake had previously loosened the tacks for her. She gathered the tacks and nails from the floor and threw them in the trash, then folded the coverings, and took the pile to the laundry room.

Izzie came back in the living room and stared at something on top of the ironing board. At the wide end, taped, was a large manila envelope with scorched edges. She removed it, gently opened the sealed flap and looked inside.

I was excited. My sweetie called me over to her as she sat down on the floor and hugged me close. Had Izzie made a startling discovery?

"Sammy, why do you think Clarabelle would have this mess of papers in her ironing board?"

Izzie did this a lot. She'd ask me a question which she knew full well I couldn't answer. Many times, I did know the answer, but poor Izzie did not understand dogspeak.

Clarabelle said her safety net was her ironing board. I didn't see any nets around the papers but what did I know about human sayings. Made sense to me to read the papers and find out. Izzie crossed her legs and leaned back against the wall. I snuggled closer against Izzie to give her some moral support.

Izzie sighed and began to examine the papers. Not to be left out I stayed cuddled beside her. To me, it looked like these were papers with Clarabelle's handwriting. These weren't the pretty birthday and Easter cards she sent through the years but sheets of paper, some wrinkled and brown around the edges.

Izzie began to read out loud. Her voice drifted. I could feel her fragile body droop. For a few seconds she was quiet, her head bowed and buried it in her hands. She trembled as she again began to read to me, then sobbed, and held me tightly as she rocked back and forth. I feared we were in for an unhappy time.

Chapter 27

Three days later we drove back to Nesbit. Izzie tucked Clarabelle's manila folder into a tweed briefcase, then grabbed her pink overnight bag and my food. This trip I brought my Teddy bear who needed a good licking, my way of cleaning the fuzzy rascal.

Olivia was home from the hospital, though still resting upstairs. Each day she caused problems, according to the calls Izzie got from Hannah. Olivia fired two caregivers because one didn't iron her lounging gown before she dressed in the morning and the other one because she neglected to cut off all the crusts of Olivia's grilled pimento cheese sandwich.

"Mother was never an easy person to live with, but this takes the cake," Izzie said to me as we drove.

I wasn't sure where we were taking the cake. I actually hadn't seen Izzie put a cake in the car. I was sniffing Daisy before we left so I could've missed it. We drove into the driveway of Olivia's house as Hannah brought groceries in from her car.

I smelled chicken. It was those yummy, juicy ones the Colonel cooks. I believe he's from another state. Many times, I heard Izzie say she was going to Kentucky Colonels for chicken. We settled in the kitchen for, as Hannah said, a bite of lunch. I never understood this bite business. Either we eat or we don't. A bite never has been enough for me. Hey, I'm not complaining 'cause I got several bites as the sisters talked about how to handle Mother.

After the sisters finished their bite of lunch, Hannah carried Olivia's lunch tray upstairs. Izzie was cleaning the kitchen when I heard someone outside. Izzie looked out the window over the sink when I started to bark. I hadn't realized it was Uncle Jessie until he strode past me with some smelly red flowers. They made my eyes water like when I'd been in the swimming pool. I hid under a kitchen chair until he was out of the room and headed upstairs, then listened for Olivia to sneeze, but heard nothing. I guess she liked them. Hannah came in the kitchen as Izzie loaded the dishwasher with their lunch dishes.

"Mom wasn't through with lunch, so we'll need to get her tray later. Thought I'd give them a chance to visit."

"Jessie whizzed past me like he had no time for small talk, nor a causal greeting, and headed for the stairs. Haven't they talked lately?"

"No, not since she got home day before yesterday. According to the nurses, several who thought him darlin', he was at the hospital several times. One night he brought his guitar and sang for Mom. They thought him dreamy, so Nurse Betty Jo told me."

"I'm not surprised. Hey, what time does the new caregiver come in?"

"She'll be here any minute. This is another new one. I'll have to break her in gently to learn Mother's way of doing things. She said on her application she played Mah Jongg, so that's a plus. Maybe she'll join mother and the ladies on their Thursday Mah Jongg game. She'll be here until nine o'clock tonight. Why don't you talk to her?"

"Oh, no, you'll not get me tangled in this mess," Izzie said.

"How about we talk to her together. I need support."

"Okay. I need to call Jake. I'll be in the den. Come get me when she gets here."

Our lunch was over. There was nothing for me to do so I laid my tummy on the cool marble floor in the entry hall outside the kitchen door. I could see the front door open as the sisters greeted a large, gray-haired lady in pink, flowered scrubs. I wanted to bark, tell her pink flowers were not her best style but decided my opinion should stay with me.

The sisters talked for a while with Pink Flowers. When the three ladies went in the kitchen Izzie said she'd pop in, say hi to her mother and get the lunch tray. I watched as Hannah reached into the cupboard beside the stove for glasses.

Pink Flowers picked up the small bone-handled knife and began to half the lemons, scraping the seeds into the sink. Hannah turned on the juicer and held a lemon to it. I watched as the juice dropped into a clear glass bowl. The smell tickled my nose and caused me to sneeze. The yummy lemonade was special when Hannah used mint from the garden. I left them with the juicer machine whirling its shrill sound. Shrill sounds are not my thing.

This was my clue to go upstairs. The staircase was long and curved but I ran upstairs with ease. I snooped through the five bedrooms and three baths. Nothing to hold my interest. I finally settled on a soft velvety loveseat outside Olivia's bedroom.

My eyelids shut, then sprang open. Uncle Jessie was talking in a muttered level I couldn't understand. Better move, I thought, to be in a better listening position. I found a dark corner behind a floral dressing screen to see, but not to be seen. Uncle Jessie held Olivia's hand as he sat by her on the apple-green velvet fainting couch.

He held her gaze and whispered. From the corner of my eye I saw Izzie ease up the stairs. She approached her mother's bedroom door, then stopped abruptly when she heard Jessie's voice.

Chapter 28

"Love is the only word I can use." Jessie leaned in toward Olivia. "Ya' feel it too, I know ya' do. At least, ya' used to. I've loved ya' since the day we met at your eighteenth birthday party. Matt and I came together. I led the partygoers in Happy Birthday. Our eyes met and I was hooked. Businessman, Matt, visited with your dad that day while we stole some time alone."

I changed my position on the carpet behind the dressing screen to get a better view of Jessie and Olivia and still watched Izzie standing in the hall. My ears pricked at what I heard next.

"Matt was so much like my father." Olivia adjusted her toe length silk robe as she lay on her fainting couch. "Life was serious to him. Both worked in the construction business and wanted the money and prestige that came from their dedication to work. I was a kid. I wanted to have fun. You were a jokester. We had a wild and crazy spring and summer. The problem was I drank too much at the Fourth of July Barbeque. I made a mistake when I had sex with Matt that one night. Jessie, our relationship was ruined after that mistake with him. All hell broke loose when I told my folks."

"Remember, ya' didn't want to marry Matt," Jessie said. "I knew then I was your true love. I didn't blame ya' then, not now. What could ya' do? That damned Matt was hell bent on making an honest woman out of ya'. Little did they know ya' were carrying my child."

Izzie, still standing in the hallway put her hands to her mouth. I was hidden behind the dressing screen, unable to get to her without being seen.

"Your father," Jessie continued, "wanted the wedding, knowing Matt was becoming a prosperous businessman. I wasn't a catch then. Still a cock-fighter with a guitar. If only ya'd been brave enough to listen to me."

"I wanted to marry you, too, Jessie. I truly did, but I was young and afraid. You remember, my dad was a very persuasive person and he had reasons to want Matt in his family."

"I couldn't get over ya'." Jessie gently kissed the hand he held. "You were the reason my music improved. Through my music my broken heart gave me the venue to express myself. Even in heartache, ya' were my inspiration." He leaned closer and kissed her forehead. "I couldn't find anyone else to love, ya've always been my soul-mate no matter what has happened to us."

Olivia drew back and flipped her long blonde curls behind her ear. "You and Father Sims seemed to get along pretty well."

Jessie dropped her hand. "Ya' know that connection was just sex for both of us. Men friends. Our bond started a long time before I knew ya'. My feelings are built-in to me. I knew I was bi-sexual from when I was a kid. Father Sims was only a few years older when the bishop assigned him to our parish. Singing was my outlet and he nourished my talent. God-given, he said. I chose that relationship freely." Jessie's gaze moved toward the window, then back to Olivia.

"He befriended me as a teenager. Had it not been for Father Sims, my life would've taken a long, dark path directly to prison. He would have been excommunicated. To be with another woman seemed like a betrayal to you, yet with Timothy Sims, I felt free to show my emotions, my frustrations. Sometimes sex was the only answer to that frustration. We were what the other needed."

"Do you think it was his body they found in the church?" Olivia asked.

"Oh, yes, I know it was."

"How can you be sure? Haven't you been in Memphis? I don't understand how you can be so sure."

"Olivia, Darling," Jessie patted her hand. "I had to take care of him like I did Matt. Father Sims was going to confess to the bishop the secret we'd shared since I was a teenager. He couldn't shake the memory. He kept remembering what I had to do to avenge my pa. I had no choice. I had to kill a smart-ass kid. Just like with Matt. Ya' told me what Matt did to ya'. I had to protect ya' forever from his drunkenness."

"I told you we were both drinking." Olivia's voice edged higher. "I didn't mean for you to react so violently. I wanted to be assured you still loved me after having a second child. I couldn't stand to think I'd lost you after another foolish night."

"No, no, I had to even the score with him, even if he was my brother. Remember the loan he'd promised me for that record demo? Remember he got to the bank, then changed his mind? Ya' have no idea how embarrassed I was. That was the same week ya' told me about that New Year's Eve rape. I'd had enough. I did what I had to do for us both."

I turned toward the hallway to see my sweet momma wiping tears from her cheeks with the back of her hand. Her eyes were red and glassy. As Mr. Perry Mason would say 'the clues now began to fit'.

"Had you planned to do that to Father Sims?" she asked.

"No, not really. It just fell into place. I knew what would happen if he continued to talk about his last confession. He was more ill than most knew. Every time we saw each other Sims was hung-up on the idea of a last confession to the Bishop. He was obsessed with guilt." Jessie squinted and frowned. "I finally realized he would eventually confess."

"You've always been so kind, so gentle with me. I can't hear this. I feel like I'm talking to another person, one I don't know. It's hard to believe you've committed these acts."

"It was really pretty simple. We'd had Clarabelle's funeral earlier that day. We were sitting having a few drinks and again, like at the funeral lunch, Sims brought up his health and how he needed to make a confession. I was outraged at the funeral lunch, but had calmed down by evening, or so I thought. As the evening progressed, the more he talked about clearing his conscience, the angrier I became. I tried to reason with him that his sins, like mine, were paybacks to those who had harmed us. These were people the law would never bring to justice. He wasn't buying that, so I changed the subject.

"I asked Father Sims about the new generator he'd bought for the church, saying I might need one for my place in Memphis. He offered to show it to me. Though we could have walked, we rode to the church in his truck. That one decision turned out to be an advantage for me.

I had earlier loaded some of my tools in his truck to fix a leaky water pipe. I grabbed the hammer as we got out of the truck, followed him into the church. He walked ahead of me. I gave him a little push as we started down the stairs, then finished him off with the hammer and drug the body into the kitchen. It was easy to gather up some kitchen rags, pour gasoline on them, then start the fire."

Jessie leaned toward Olivia and hugged her. This was my chance to slip out of the room unnoticed. I ran straight to the hall, to my sweetie, now wiping her puffy eyes. A flash came to my brain. I remembered the hammer I found and why it was important. It was, as Perry Mason would've said, a clue. Clues fuse actions together in order to solve the puzzle. Now the puzzle could be solved.

"But, you were in Memphis or that's what the Sheriff said when he was around asking all of us questions"

"Of course, I wasn't going to stick around. I drove his truck to the rectory, loaded my Harley in the bed and drove to the lake. I parked heading it into the water, so the tailgate was nearly touching the ground, backed the Harley out of the bed and headed to Memphis."

Olivia gasped. "No. My love. What have you done?"

Izzie quietly fled down the staircase grasping the handrail for support. At the foot of the stairs, she bumped into Pink Flower who was headed out to the garden. She had Olivia's mint basket over her arm. Hannah had said it was a family tradition to put mint in her lemonade and sweet tea.

Still a young guy at the time I tore down those steps as fast as my short legs could carry me. Izzie dashed into the hall bathroom, slammed the door. I heard that same sound I've heard before when she came home late. I scratched at the door as fast as I could.

Nothing, then I heard a flushing sound.

Chapter 29

Izzie slowly opened the powder room door. I looked at my Sweetie in disbelief. Her eyes were red, glassy. Her hair rumpled, and the front of her shirt was wet. My sweetie was a mess. She staggered down the hall into the kitchen. Hannah turned from the kitchen sink.

"What's the matter with you, Izzie? You look pale as a ghost. Why were you upstairs so long? Where's Mother's tray?"

Izzie glanced around the kitchen, walked to the back door, shut and locked it. "Oh my God, I'm sick to my stomach."

I raced to her as she sat in a chair at the kitchen table.

"Please give me some water. You'll never believe what I just heard Uncle Jessie say."

"What was it? Tell me."

"I think he killed our daddy, and maybe Father Sims, and there's more."

"No, that doesn't make any sense. He's Daddy's brother."

"You're right, but this info goes along with what I'd found in

Clarabelle's letter to us. Let's stay calm until he leaves, then I'll read you the letter."

"I want Patrick here too. If this came from his grandmother, he should hear it."

"That goes for Jake. We could use his input as well as—

The sound of someone coughing as they came down the stairs made both girls gasp mid-sentence and look at each other. A brief moment later Jessie came into the kitchen.

"Gotta run girls. Gotta audition at five o'clock. Take care. I'll see ya' later."

Just like that, he was out the back door and gone. Pink Flowers came in from the garden with sweet smelling mint. Hannah sent her upstairs to get the tray, followed close behind to make the necessary introduction. I had no idea what happened upstairs with the new caregiver, but she and Olivia were laughing as Hannah, in contrast, came in the kitchen crying. Izzie hugged her sister. Hannah's crying slowed to sobs.

"Mother's lounging in her bedroom, talking and visiting with Flora like they are old friends," Hannah muttered. "It's like she heard nothing Jessie said. Mother is so insensitive. This is one time I thought she'd be upset and find fault with the caregiver. Instead, she's chatting with her like two old hens having a gossip party."

"I'll go on to Jake's," Izzie said. "We can talk freely there. You pick up Patrick and come on over when you can."

"I'll call him now. We'll be at Jake's as soon as we can."

Chapter 30

The sun was nearly gone for the day when Hannah and Patrick opened Jake's screen door. Buddy ran in ahead of them and headed for our water bowl. Same as always, water slurped on the floor. Izzie set out some brie and crackers while I ate my supper. Buddy cleaned the bowl after I had my fill.

Jake removed four short, squatty glasses from the cabinet. Ice cubes clunked against the sides. The coke he added next made a sizzling sound of bubbles popping. One-time Jake put his glass on the floor, I investigated, took a sniff, and those bubbles attacked my nose. I prefer water.

Izzie rubbed the nap of her neck and frowned. Her eyes, still swollen, stared ahead, looking at no one in particular.

"We've gathered here for two reasons. Hannah and I feel it important we are together to hear what I have to say. Everyone here will be affected in some way by this information. First, I will read the letter Clarabelle wrote for Hannah and me concerning daddy's death. She hid it under the covers of her ironing board where it has been over twenty years. Guffin gave the ironing board to me to make a table, never realizing what lay under the padding."

I don't remember much that was said except I could tell Izzie was close to her dark place as she told about the letter and began to relay Jessie's conversation with their Mother. She still hadn't told Hannah everything she'd heard Jessie admit to.

"After I read the letter, I'll share with you the conversation I overheard between Uncle Jessie and Mother."

Buddy and I found comfortable places to rest our sluggish bodies and listened. Izzie took the stained pages from the envelope and began to read.

April 2, 1983

My name is Clarabelle Guffin, wife of Mac Guffin. I write this for my girls, Hannah and Izzie 'bout their daddy and what I saw. Tho I call you my girls, I knows you're not my birth babies, but I love you just as if you are.

I haft to write what I saw yesterday before I forget, tho I'll never forget that horrible sight. I knows I won't be believed cause of who I am, but I knows what I saw so I put it on this paper just so someday my darlin's will know the truth.

Yesterday I's going to the library taken Mr. Matt and Izzie some ginger snaps. I heard a snap, a pop. Going round the corner into the hallway I's heard 'nother, same sound. It's then I seen dis man run out the library room and out da back door.

I's only seen the side of his face coming out the door, but I seen nough to know him. Anyways I know that buckskin jacket. As I stared, the sun lit on his cock belt buckle. Then I knows for sure I seen Mr. Jessie. As God is my witness and on my blessed momma's grave, I seen Mr. Jessie, your daddy's brother, run from that room.

Oh, Lordy, the mess in that room I'll never forget. Mr. Matt, out of his wheelchair, on the floor in a pool of blood, blood all over de place. Precious Izzie on the floor. Little puppy Stella whimpering behind the sofa.

I don't know who called who cause I was holdin' little Izzie in my arms. People were all around. Since I'd heard two pops I's sure you were shot too. I was scared I'd lost you.

Someone says you were passed out, then in a coma. You've never woke up all night. Miss Olivia and I were with you till early this mornin' when those doctors sent us home. He said it could take a long time for you to come round but I's going back after I get things settled here. Your Momma's got all them funeral things to take care of. I'll not leave you tills you wake, no matter how long it takes. Poor Hannah, you all scared and confused but yo Momma will see no harm comes to you.

My heart aches for your loss. Mr. Matt was feared by some, but I saw the sadness many times in his eyes. He was a kind and generous man to me and my family, and he loved you sweet things as good or better than any daddy I knows.

God bless you sweet darlins. Yo knows I write this from my love for you. I holds you close in my heart till my dyin' day and beyond.

Your true and faithful friend, Clarabelle

Izzie sat quietly. Clarabelle's letter lay in her lap. Not a word was spoken by anyone. I licked Izzie's hand. Buddy snored.

Chapter 31

No one spoke. They sat in silent shock and disbelief. I know about shock and disbelief. It's the emotion I felt when the kitty turned out to be one of those smelly things with an enormous black and white tail that farts a lot.

"Oh, my God!" Hannah tears glistened on her face. "This is crazy. In my wildest dreams I would not have guessed this. I had some doubt when Izzie shared some of the information she'd heard from Jessie. Now we know for sure what happened. This letter backs up the gruesome facts Izzie heard today."

"I'm sure we believe grandmother's letter." Patrick stood and paced the floor, then sat down beside Hannah. "But this isn't enough to prove someone's guilt. She's not here to be questioned. Any lawyer worth his salt could tear this letter apart. Wasn't Sheriff Henshaw the bass player some years back in Jessie's band? Just saying, I believe there's more information we need to know before we take this to the authorities."

"There is more, much more," murmured Izzie. Jake moved closer beside her, pulled her close and gave her shoulders a gentle hug.

I could tell by the tone in my sweetie's voice she was having a hard time with what she was about to say. Sometimes in her dark place, she trembles. She was trembling now. She spoke in jagged sentences as she told them the rest of what she'd heard Jessie say.

"I was standing in the hallway outside Mother's bedroom, listening. Uncle Jessie was talking about when they were young and in love. I'll get to that later. Mother asked if he thought the body found in the church could be Father Sim's. Jessie answered he knew it was the priest because he had to take care of him like he did Matt.

Hannah quickly inhaled. Patrick grabbed her hand.

Jessie said Father Sims was about to confess to the bishop the secret they'd shared when they were teenagers. He said it was like with Matt. When she told him what Matt had done, he felt he had to protect her. Mother didn't mean for Jessie to react so violently. She wanted to be assured he still loved her.

When I think about it," Hannah frowned. "Uncle Jessie has always been around us at holidays and special parties. We never knew why before now."

Izzie interrupted. "Jessie then told Mother he drove the priest's truck to the rectory, loaded his Harley in the bed and drove to the lake. He said it was parked heading into the water, so he could let the tailgate down and his *Harley* out of the truck bed. He then headed to Memphis."

Hannah gasped. "This is unbelievable."

Izzie's hands gripped her elbows. I quietly scooted against her side to give my support. My sweet Momma revealed the information about Hannah being Jessie's daughter. Hannah made an odd gasping sound and slumped against Patrick.

I don't believe it," Hannah finally spoke. "This man is a murderer. He can't be my dad, not my daddy. My daddy is Matt."

"Hannah, think about this a minute. Jessie was much more attentive to you than he ever was to me. He was always partial to you, coming to all your parties with crazy, fun gifts."

"No more than a lot of the family friends," Hannah replied. "Mr. Rocco was always there for Jake, helping him through college and buying him that horse for his sixteenth."

As Hannah spoke I saw Jake look down and run his hands through his hair. His face revealed an odd human expression, one I didn't remember seeing before. In that brief second my imagination ran to thoughts of Jake's demeanor when Izzie was close. Those ideas puzzled my doggie brain.

"There are DNA tests. We could try to get a sample of his saliva, or maybe a strand of hair would do," added Patrick. "This is a lot for each of us absorb, especially you, Hannah. It's a double whammy for you. Let's think this out. We know there isn't enough evidence to go to the authorities. Is there more we could find out? Then there's Grandmother's death. Could there be a chance Jessie had a reason to get revenge on her too?"

"Remember," Izzie chimed in. "Clarabelle said she had to hang up the phone. She said it looked like Father Sim's truck had pulled into her driveway."

"So," said Patrick, "if Father Sims told Jessie about her confession, then, I'd say that in Jessie's twisted mind, he'd have plenty of reason to want her out of the way. I'm not even sure Guffin is clearly out of the picture. The police keep calling Grandad in for the questioning. They always say it's for the last time. I wonder, at this point, if they would even give us the time of day."

The four talked about ways to learn more about Jessie's activities. My eyes began to close. Buddy snored softly. I rested against his back for enough time to start my dream about chasing those stinky, barn cats. I was brought out of the chase hearing Izzie cough, then clear her throat.

"I've got an idea. Mother will be coming downstairs in the next few days. We all know she's always up for a party, especially if it's about her. We could have a little dinner party to celebrate her improvement from the fall, ask Jessie to come, put a recorder under the dining room table and try to catch him saying something incriminating."

"I can't face him," Hannah said. "How can I sit at a table, make small talk and hold myself together thinking he might be my real father? The experience will be more difficult knowing he may have killed the man I loved as my father."

"The same way we all would," said Izzie. "There's enough sadness among the four of us to push anyone off the deep end, but what good would that do? If he's done what I know I heard him say, then everything we suspect of him is true. We have to be strong and get enough proof to go to the authorities."

"I'll go for it," said Jake.

"Count me in," Patrick said.

Izzie stood, opened her arms and raised her chin. "I'll do the planning if one of you guys will call Jessie to issue the invitation. That is, unless he pops in like he did today. In that case, whoever is at Mother's house must do the inviting."

"I'll call him," said Jake. "If he shot my dad I want to keep an eye on the bastard every minute he's around here."

Hannah said the new caregiver had taken over all the meals and had pleased her mother this evening. She would ask her, Pink Flower, to help plan the menu and prepare the meal. They continued talking about Patrick setting up the recorder and how they would try to get info out of Jessie. All I could think about was seeing those bright pink flowers floating around the formal dining room. Oh well, Buddy and I would probably be under the table and not have to look at her. Right now, I saw Buddy head for our doggie door.

I followed.

Chapter 32

For the next three days the girls were busy talking, crying, and planning for Olivia's event. They also began making friends with the new caregiver, Pink Flowers. They prayed she might stay on to take over the kitchen once she wasn't needed full-time waiting on Olivia.

I heard Izzie on the phone, she said she had sick leave, whatever that meant. We stayed at Jake's. Buddy and I had time to plan our strategies and play in the pool with our floating fish. There was little we could do to help them plan the dinner party. I still had my job to take care of my Sweetie, to keep her safe and happy. She laughed as she tossed the ball in the pool. I believe she enjoyed the game as much as I did. My heart did little leaps of joy when I heard her laughing. I'm sure my friends in the courtyard missed me but I had work to do here with Izzie.

The next morning, after I had breakfast and did my nature duty, I was puzzled to see Izzie sitting at the breakfast table staring out the kitchen window. Jake was at the farm checking on cattle in the lower pasture. Izzie sat and stared. She sat there a long time. I had to go out the doggie door two times. She sometimes sobbed, even trembled, when in her dark place. Then she'd stop rubbing her neck, come out of it and be my happy Sweetie again. I did my begging trick, which forced her to get up and go to the pantry for my treats. Soon she was smiling. All was good.

On the night of the dinner party, I could tell tensions were high because I heard loud and rapid talking. Although everyone appeared cheerful, especially after they had martinis, they would sigh or tap their fingers on their glass as they talked. A drink always started Olivia's evening of entertaining.

I didn't know time, but the sun had set a long time back. Buddy and I had been fed and done our business outside. Ms. Pinkie, as we now called her, turned out to be a dog lover and made us liver jerky. I think I loved this woman. She had some great human traits. Anyway, everyone but Jessie was there. After two rounds of drinks, still no Jessie. As they finished those drinks the phone rang.

"Yes, we can start without you, but I'd prefer to wait. Okay, we'll start on the shrimp appetizer and wait a little longer. After all, this is a special occasion and I haven't seen you in a few days."

Hannah and Patrick huddled together as they assembled in the dining room. Jake poured the wine and they began eating those things called shrimp. Buddy and I took our usual spots under the table ready for any food that would come our way. It didn't take long before I was handed a shrimp. Thank you, no cocktail sauce. When the phone rang again, Ms. Pinkie answered and came in to tell us Jessie needed to talk to Olivia.

When Olivia came back into the dining room, her face was red, her eyes looked wildly at everyone. Her attitude had changed from cheerfulness to anger.

"Jessie won't be coming, let's get on with this dinner. He said some record company executive called to meet him at The Peabody and he needed to go. Let's hope this dinner is worth the trouble you girls went to. I could absolutely kill him sometimes."

"We all wish you would've a long time ago," muttered Izzie under her breath.

"What did you say, Izzie?"

"Nothing, Mother, just a little cough."

"On to plan two," whispered Hannah to Patrick.

"What did you say, Hannah?

"Nothing, Mother, just a little cough."

"You girls need some Robitussin."

I'd heard enough. I finished Izzie's last morsel of asparagus and headed to the kitchen.

Chapter 33

I woke the next morning, hurriedly did my downward dog and raced downstairs and out the doggie door. Sometimes I was amazed at how fast my short legs could carry me if I was in a hurry. Could have been the asparagus that made me run, if you get my drift.

By the time Izzie came downstairs Jake was using the French press machine. They smiled and talked as they drank what smelled like coffee. Buddy was still asleep on the sun porch. Not to worry, he was a little older than me. He needed his beauty sleep. I had my Greenie and headed to my water bowl when I heard a ring.

It's a good thing Jake put the sound on speaker because Patrick was talking fast. I heard his voice, but his words were not clear to me. Although I was a good listener, about that age, I was starting to have some hearing issues. Not to be alarmed. One of the signs of aging dogs is hearing loss. I had learned if I cock my head to the left I heard much better. Jake hung up and began to talk to Izzie. Buddy came wandering in, so he, too, heard what was said.

Patrick said early that morning the police came to his house and arrested Guffin for the murder of Clarabelle. The authorities determined she did not have a heart attack but was suffocated by the pillow that was found on the floor. Guffin had explained when he was first questioned that he had gotten home from a cattle delivery, then later admitted he was gambling and found her dead when he arrived home. They found this suspicious. The police said the time of death was within thirty minutes give or take from the time he stated. This information, as well as his lies, made him a suspect.

Jake stroked his black beard. "I've never heard such panic in Patrick's voice. Losing his grandmother, accepting her death, then to find out it was murder was a lot to bear. Then to have his granddad arrested for it is unthinkable. That's too much to handle with a clear mind. Patrick asked me to call Rocco who probably knows the best lawyer to handle this case. I need to make that call by nine o'clock this morning."

"Does Rocco know that many people?"

"Of course," Jake replied. "He's used more lawyers that I can name, depending on his predicament. The case that nearly got him imprisoned was evading payment of years of sales tax. I can name several times he's needed a tough attorney. Not for murder, but just about everything else you could think of."

Their conversation centered on facts they could remember about the time Clarabelle died. Izzie was clear in her memory of the blue truck Clarabelle had described. She was also clear on the time of their phone conversation. They doubted it could be Father Sims at the late hour of eleven-thirty because he is known to go to bed early. Izzie was also sure Jessie was staying at the rectory because he had come down from Memphis to practice for the big Fourth of July Barbeque party Olivia was having. As far as they could remember, Jessie always stayed with Father Sims when he came to Nesbit. They had an unspoken relationship that most of the community knew about.

"Could it be possible that someone else around here has that same-looking Dodge pick-up?" Izzie seemed cheerful she had thought of something else to pursue. "Maybe someone that was a friend of

Guffin's? Or maybe, someone he'd lost money to during one of his gambling nights?"

"I don't think so. Clarabelle knew nearly everyone around here and surely would have recognized their truck. She was talking to you when the truck drove up so I believe she would have said who it was if it were someone else."

Since those two couldn't figure it out, Buddy and I decided to go into action. He ran into Jake's bedroom, jumped on the bed, dug back the coverlet and pushed off a pillow. I followed. We started a tug-of-war as we ran back into the kitchen, each tugging and pulling on the ends until the pillowcase started to come off. A few more shakes by Buddy and with a firm tug, I pulled and off came the pillowcase.

"Look at those two," said Jake. "They can have a lot of fun being mischievous. Look, they've pulled off the pillowcase just like they had a plan in mind."

Izzie said, "Why are you standing in front of me shaking that case, my Love Sponge?"

There she goes again. She knows she can't understand dogspeak even though I was doing my very best good-natured growl. I'd shake the case some more and maybe she'd get the idea. She smiled. Maybe that meant something, like her brain had just gone into action.

"Hey, Jake." Izzie pulled the pillowcase from me. "Do you remember me telling you about the day Hannah and I straightened Clarabelle's house. We were changing the linens on both Clarabelle's and Guffin's beds and noticed something, finding it odd one of the pillowcases was missing. I remember we remarked she would never use a pillow without a case on it. We even looked for one to match the one on Guffin's bed, but it wasn't there."

"Maybe it was already put in the hamper for the laundry."

"No, it wasn't. We paid special attention as we loaded the washer. I remember the case on Guffin's bed. It had lavender tatting around the hem."

"Wait a minute," said Jake. "Wasn't there a rag or something in that satchel Buddy dropped out of Father's truck? The one that had pieces of sheet music in it?"

"You're right. Did it get tossed back in the truck bed or did the Sheriff take it? If it was on the pillow at her house, and she was suffocated, then the murderer could have taken it with him so no trace of him would be detected."

"I'll call the Sheriff now and ask. Won't take a minute and then we'll know." Jake started toward the phone.

"Wait. When I was helping Hannah put back the rug under the recliner, I distinctly remember two coke bottles. One was on the table beside her chair, the other one had rolled under the recliner. I tossed both bottles and two lids in the trash."

"Clarabelle would not have had two cokes to drink, but maybe she would've offered one to someone who had come to visit."

"And if that could be true, then one of those bottles could have the visitor's fingerprints on it. Problem is, that's been several weeks ago. I'm sure the trash is gone by now."

"Maybe not. I think I'd better call Patrick and find how often the trash is picked up."

Mission accomplished. Buddy and I retired to the sunroom for a much-needed nap. We were close enough to hear what happened next, if we could stay awake.

Chapter 34

Buddy snored as soon as his head hit the favorite bunny toy he used for a pillow. My turtle worked great for my pillow when I slept. I, on the other hand, was keenly alert to Jake's voice. He had made a phone call, I presumed he'd called to ask Patrick the question about the trash.

Wait, I was mistaken. Jake was asking questions, but not of Patrick. He'd called Rocco. From the conversation I heard, Rocco did know the perfect attorney. He was most anxious to help, especially when he said the information Jake and Izzie had not shared with anyone would be important to their attorney. It would give the attorney a better defense if he had as much info as possible.

Jake's next call was to Patrick to tell him Rocco would be in touch and willing to assist if he needed any help with the defense of his grandad.

"Patrick is on the move this morning." Jake hung up the phone. "He's already called Citizens Bank in Nashville for a loan for the defense. That's an interesting bank. I remember him telling me it was the first bank in the south founded by all black businessmen in nineteen-hundred-four. The required deposit at that time was ten cents. Patrick started banking there when he was in college in Nashville. I think he owns some stock. He said there was no question about him getting a loan."

"Did he know anything about his folk's trash pick-up?"

"That's interesting. Patrick said they didn't have a trash pick-up service. Guffin takes the trash to the dump when they get a lot of bags and when he gets around to it. There's no regular schedule. All the bags are still in the lean-two from before Clarabelle's death and none have been hauled away he knows of."

"Where would we begin to go through all those bags?" Izzie tightened the band around her ponytail.

"Listen to me, Little Lady. This is police business. I'll call them with the facts, then we'll see what they do with the info."

Jake made the call which took such a long time I was able to run to the sunroom to wake Buddy. We were coming into the kitchen as he hung up.

"The department was interested in your pillowcase theory but didn't act very happy about going through all those bags of trash."

Not to take anything away from my Sweetie, but what did he mean her theory? Who does he think gave her the pillowcase idea? Guess I'd better leave well enough alone and be grateful she paid attention because Buddy and I have more to share later. Izzie opened the oven door to remove something that smelled like eggs and sausage. She called this concoction a breakfast casserole.

My Teddy's belly was getting a good licking when I heard the purr of Hannah's Jag as she pulled into the driveway. I decided I'd give her a friendly bark. She came in the kitchen and gave my ears a much-needed scratch. That sausage smelled so tempting I would've jumped on the counter if my legs were long enough. Izzie gave her sister a tight hug as she came in the kitchen and poured them both a cup of coffee.

Jake filled his dented green water thermos and headed out the back door.

"Ladies I'll leave this mess with the two of you to solve. The guys are moving cattle to the feed lot today and I need to check on them. I'll be gone a couple hours. Save some breakfast casserole for me."

The door shut with a bang. Hannah began to cry. Izzie leaned over from her chair to comfort her sister. Instead, she knocked over both cups of coffee. The table and floor offered me nothing I cared to lick, so I left the cleaning to the girls.

"Oh dear, I'm such a klutz."

She didn't need to remind us. Anyone who knew and loved her, already knew this.

Hannah frowned. "Don't worry. Let's just clean up this mess. Izzie, I don't know what we should do first. Try to find out if Jessie really is my father or just turn him in to the police."

"This is for you to decide." Izzie wiped the table with damp paper towels. "Remember, we all agreed we have no proof of his guilt. It would be the letter and my word against his. I did relay our experience about the pillowcase to Jake and he told Patrick and the police. If Jessie was with Father Sims and they drove to the church for whatever reason, then Jessie could have driven the truck to the lake hauling his motorcycle in the bed. That would explain why his sheet music and the pillowcase were found in the satchel. He was in a hurry to get away and simply forgot them."

"You said motorcycle tracks were behind the bed of the truck and the truck was definitely Father's. This would've been an easy way for Jessie to get back to Memphis. Leaving the Dodge at the lake caused everyone to think Father had committed suicide or wandered off."

"What," Izzie asked "if the item we thought was a rag turns out to be the pillowcase with the lavender tatting? Then we have a connection of both the murders to Jessie, not Guffin."

My tail began to wag. It was that tap, tap wag. The sisters got it. This was exactly what Buddy and I were trying to tell them.

Chapter 35

The sisters talked and planned while Buddy and I went outside to play our pool game. This time we had a problem. I smelled a raccoon, unusual, he normally showed himself at dusk. He was probably the same one I'd spied washing a shiny green frog in the pool last week. Buddy and I were out to catch him, but we couldn't find him around any of the bushes. Where had that little raccoon devil gone? We were running to check around the cabana when Izzie called me. Better luck next time. We were getting in her car to leave when Jake drove up.

"You leaving, Izzie? You gals make your plans? Did I interrupt anything important?"

"Sammy and I were just leaving, so you're back just in time," said Izzie. "We think we have a plan to record or transmit Jessie's confession."

"You'd better be careful. He's not likely to just come out and confess anything to either of you, especially Hannah."

"Not to worry. I'll be the one talking to him," said Izzie. "I'm asking him to the boat for a drink to discuss a surprise birthday party for Mother."

"I'll be back on the dock. In case anything goes wrong I can call the cops. I'll not be near the boat," said Hannah. "I was starting to call Patrick to ask him to be there with me when you came in. I'll call him while Izzie explains our plan to you."

"I'd better be hiding somewhere near or maybe on the boat for your safety, Izzie."

"Not a bad idea, but where? You could go behind the door in the bow next to the bunk beds. He'd have no reason to go in there. I could open the porthole in case you had to get out in a hurry. We commonly have it open for light and fresh air. She opened the car door. I jumped in the back. Gotta leave. If you can drive up tomorrow I'll explain more."

"I'll be there by noon and bring us some lunch." Jake winked at us as he hopped out of the Jeep.

Izzie and I left Jake's and drove north to Memphis.

The twenty-one-mile drive on I-55 N took only twenty minutes that day. I know this because Izzie remarked to me, "I put the pedal to the metal. I can't tell time, but I know the trip was short because I didn't finish my chew bone before we were in Memphis.

Chapter 36

Izzie arrived home from her night shift in time to save me. I should never get up during the night for a drink. My trip down the elevator was fun because both Daisy and Sabbath rode with me. We ran out the elevator into a bright sunny morning. It was going to be another muggy summer day, for sure. My pals had no idea a thrilling day lay ahead for me. Izzie and I were going to catch the bad guy.

Well, that was the plan.

Daisy started to dig up the nice big bone Sabbath buried last week but he laid one of his big paws on her back and gave her a push. Not an aggressive type of dog, I decided it safer to follow Izzie back upstairs and leave the troublemakers to themselves.

I finished my Greenie and snuggled up to Izzie on the sofa while she had a little shut eye. I was ready to lunge for the black and white barn cat with the fuzzy tail when I heard a knock on the door. Izzie didn't budge. I started whining as the second knock got louder. This couldn't be Jake already. He wasn't supposed to be here till noon.

I whined louder. Izzie struggled to her feet, then tripped over my Teddy bear. She caught herself on the coffee table and stumbled to the door. It was Jake and Buddy. Buddy ran past me straight to my water dish. He was finally satisfied after making a sloppy mess of water on the kitchen floor. I prayed Izzie didn't slip in it.

Several little white cartons of good smells came from the sack Jake was carrying. I smelled Thai. It must've been noon. Guess we got more than a little shut eye. No matter, I craved that smell.

Jake gave Izzie a big hug. "I brought Thai from the Purple Orchid. Go wash your sleepy face while I set the table."

Izzie smiled back and hurried toward the bathroom.

She was back in a flash, gently placed her hand on his forearm. "You always know what's best, anything red curry and coconut milk. I am so hungry I could eat the carton. Wait, I'll get the chopsticks."

Izzie called those rice dishes curry or curvy, not sure which. Not my favorite spice but the chicken was always good. I really wish she'd stick to steak, rare, if you please, with a few bites of asparagus.

My tummy, round and full, rested next to Buddy on the cool stone kitchen floor. Time for a short nap. The door creaked as it opened and shut. Izzie and Jake were gone. Eyelids heavy, muscles limp. Dream time.

Chapter 37

The front door slammed. Buddy and I had slept all afternoon but now raced to greet our family. We wagged and barked which signaled our need to piddle. Izzie opened the door and we ran into the hall while Jake put his finger on the wall button. Magically the elevator door opened. We hopped in.

We all rode the elevator down to the courtyard. Izzie and Jake sat on a bench in the shade while we took care of nature's call. My Doberman friend, Sabbath, was not happy having Buddy around. Don't underestimate Buddy, he can be pretty sharp sometimes. He sniffed around the courtyard until he found just what he needed. An old tennis ball was under an azalea plant. Buddy grabbed it and ran over and dropped it in front of Sabbath. Sabbath gave some sniffs of approval, then off we were. We romped and played with that old ball until our tongues were hanging.

Playtime over, we rode up to the fourth floor while Izzie and Jake chattered about that day's meeting with the police. I wanted to know more about that meeting, but they talked less when we reached our floor. I'm sure they realized it was time for my supper 'cause I ran straight to my food bowl and whined. Buddy got his supper too. He gulped his food so fast I don't think he tasted it.

That evening Izzie did a lot of phone talking. I heard her say she would see them tomorrow, late afternoon. She was all smiles as she popped a big pan of something Italian in the oven. Yes, it was Italian. I knew the smell of garlic. My nose was very keen in my younger days.

Buddy snored. I stretched and curled against him. Jake poured Izzie red wine. It was a good night. My doggie brain told me tomorrow, late afternoon, would be very different.

Chapter 38

Grey clouds covered the sun as we drove to the Memphis docks on Mud Island. Thunder rumbled in the distance as Izzie parked the car in the lot of the Memphis Yacht Club. When we left the loft, Jake had been in his Jeep behind us. I didn't see him out the back window for the last few blocks. Maybe he got caught in traffic. We walked to the cruiser at the Mud Island Marina, the fish-tainted smell of the river around us, Izzie with a sack of groceries, me on my leash.

Earlier I overheard Izzie and Jake go over her list of topics to bring up to Jessie. Still, no Jake to be seen. I spotted a yellow fuzzy cat, tugged on my leash and started to bark. "Stop that, Sammy. Hurry now, I have things to do before Jessie arrives."

When we got on the cruiser Momma unhooked my leash, put me in my yellow life vest, filled my water bowl and gave me a chewy bone. She went to the bow where the bunk beds were located. She opened the porthole with a loud snap. I never saw what else she did 'cause I was busy watching people as I stood on the sofa. I put my paws on the window frame and got a real good look at who came and went.

Izzie set out some cheese dip and crackers, then took a bottle of a purple liquid she called grape juice and poured half of it into the decanter she usually used for red wine.

"Jake should've been here by now. Where could he be? Maybe he got caught in the street construction. I hope not."

I thought the same thing. The last thing we needed was to face Jessie alone. I knew I could protect my Sweetie, but I'm more of a lover than a fighter.

"Jessie will never think I'm drinking grape juice because he always wants Guinness. I hope this twelve pack is enough. I'll go ahead and pour myself a glass in case he comes early. He'll reason I've already started. He may think I'm in a daze, but I want my brain clear when I talk to the SOB."

I had no idea what or who SOB was. Maybe someone was coming I didn't know. I hopped off the sofa, ran to get a drink, and saw Izzie attach a small box to the bottom of the sofa where I had been resting. I watched with ears alert. Not a sound came from the little box. She, Jake, Hannah, and Patrick must have made more plans after I fell asleep yesterday. I didn't remember any talk about tiny boxes.

Izzie bent down to the floor, knelt on her hands and knees and slid another box under the sofa. She then patted the sofa. "Get back up here and lay down, Sammy. I want you here on the sofa. The flounce will hide any evidence of the radio transmitter I've placed under it. The transmitter will broadcast our conversion back to the police on shore. Uncle Jessie would never sit here to pet you. This way, he is across from us as he speaks."

"Look at me, Sammy," she continued. "Listen. Momma may need to talk hateful to you today. If I do, get off this sofa and follow me. Don't bark back at me, just follow me. Understand?"

I know when Izzie says 'look at her' I am to listen very carefully. I cocked my head sideways left to let all her words soak in.

Izzie was coming out of the head when I heard someone jump on the boat. I started to bark but Izzie hushed me with a stern expression. I got quiet, wagged my tail, and lay on the sofa like Momma told me to do. Jessie came through the door with a bottle of red stuff and a box. We had a problem. No Jake.

Chapter 39

"Brought ya' some wine, pretty young lady." Jessie came through the cabin door, kissed Izzie on the cheek and set a box of Mrs. See's candy on the table.

For a second or two Izzie's face flushed. Her eyes widened and her mouth twisted. She seemed baffled, either by that startling kiss or the wine.

I stared at the box of candy on the table. I had a good sniffer, this box of candy didn't smell like the chocolate Izzie usually brought home. After another whiff I still got no chocolate smell. Odd, I thought. The only sniff I got was of Uncle Jessie.

"That's so thoughtful of you, Uncle Jessie. Since I've already started, I'll finish the wine I decanted earlier then start on yours." Izzie gave him her little-fake-smile and turned toward the refrigerator. "Care for a Guinness?"

"Sounds good to me." Jessie plopped down on the wing-back across from me. "So, what's this we need to talk about? Oh, yes, Olivia's birthday party next month. First, let me tell you why I missed your mother's get-well party. I thought I'd get away sooner that evening but the producer I met at The Peabody did some serious talkin'. I was so nervous when he called for the meeting I couldn't find any of my original songs to show him. But he's willin' to promote me for a show in Vegas. Can ya believe it? Poor Uncle Jessie on the strip in the big lights? Right up there with Tom Jones."

"Yes, I can believe it. You've got a great voice and it's time you were recognized for the things you do, have done." Izzie handed him his beer and sat down beside me. I heard a hint of sarcasm in Izzie's voice. "Good vocal cords must run in the family. Hannah has such a pure pitch when she sings, she must get it from you. Daddy was never much of a singer, although he did whistle a tune now and then."

"Yeah, when we were teenagers, Father Sims tried to help us both, but I was the only one with any real talent. Got this voice from my ma. It took lots of practice to find my voice. Man, I'm thirsty. It's muggy in this cabin. Why don't we start the engine and take her out a ways? We could probably get some of Ol' Mississippi breeze."

"I'd rather not. I think we're okay here."

"Ah, come on." Jessie's voice was more cynical. "Humor your Uncle Jessie this once. I'm sure we'll be better off a little ways from shore. Ya' start her up now and find us a breeze."

Izzie stood, moved at a snail's pace to comply with his demand. I wondered how Jake could help us if we were away from shore. Jessie untied the ropes releasing us from the shore. Too late. We were on our own. He staggered back in the cabin all smiles. The motor hummed as we floated into Wolf River Harbor, then moved slowly toward Joe Curtis Point and Beale Street Landing. We headed into the Mississippi, probably a half mile from shore.

I was a little bit afraid what Jessie would do next. We were away from anyone who could help us.

"I'm dropping anchor at Big River Crossing. Jessie, will you drop it? I'll get you another beer and pour myself some wine. I agree, you were right. It's cooler out here away from shore."

"See, your old Uncle has a good idea now and then. I wanted to tell ya—

Izzie interrupted. "We were talking about Father Sims a while ago." She glanced toward the shore as she came to sit beside me. "You two have been close since those early days. What do you make of his murder?"

Jessie stopped talking mid-sentence. For a few seconds he paused, licked his lips, and shifted his eye contact from Izzie to the floor. That sudden change in his demeanor frightened me. I could smell his sweat. Was he thinking how to answer?

"Sometimes the Lord takes those who need to go."

"I don't think the Lord, as you put it, needs to take a good soul like Father by murder," Izzie snapped back. "Do you?"

"I don't suppose ya' knew. Father Sims had stage four lung cancer. His time was going to be short. His death might've spared him a lot of pain."

"He didn't have time to give his last confession. Surely, the Lord would say he needed that. Still, does anything justify murder? Maybe some things do. What do you think? I can't believe it was to rid him the pain cancer would cause."

"Yeah, I feel ya're right, he would've tried or wanted to make that last confession." Jessie chugged down the last of his beer.

Izzie quickly produced another bottle from the fridge, picked up a couple crackers, and poured herself some more purple liquid. I got a scratch as she sat beside me.

"If I were to guess," Izzie rubbed her palms together. "I'd say the same goes for Clarabelle. As pious as she was she, too, was denied that last wish. I guess you know the police don't think she had a massive heart attack. Funny, I was talking to her the night she died. She said she had to hang up, Father Sims truck had just driven in her driveway. I said it couldn't be Father. It was after eleven o'clock and everyone knows he's turned in by nine o'clock."

"Don't know nothin' about that. Maybe in her condition she began seeing things."

"You mentioned you couldn't find your songs which I do admit you've got quite a knack for writing. It must be thrilling to put your thoughts, your heartaches on paper, then hear them sung. I've heard you're getting known as the guy to go to for a good emotional song."

I laid on the sofa not moving a muscle. I was like frozen, afraid to move, wondering what was going to be said.

Izzie leaned back on the sofa, next to me and tilted her head. "I was wondering, you said you lost a brown satchel full of sheet music?"

She started to work her charm. She grinned her fake smile. When she squinted her eyes and curled lip I knew my Izzie was up to something. I'd heard her say she could accomplish a lot when she fed the ego. I thought, yes, Jessie would fall for words, but I preferred a bone.

"Yeah, maybe. I can't remember if they were in my brown satchel or not. I looked around the house. I couldn't find them when I met the guy from Vegas."

"I know where they are, if you want them."

"Sure do. I'd be grateful if ya' have them. There's a heap of work there. Some of my songs date back to when Hannah was a baby. I can't imagine trying to redo all them tunes. Ya say ya know where they are? I'd be relieved to find them."

"No problem. You tell me how your music got in Father Sim's truck then I'll tell you." Izzie sat up straight and made direct eye contact with Jessie. "Or, you could march your fat ass up to the police station in

Nesbit, confess your crimes and maybe they'll just hand your songs over to you right there, if they don't arrest you first."

"See here, girlie, watch your tone. You don't know who you're dealing with. What do mean ya' saw it? Where did ya' see my music?"

"I saw your music and the pillowcase you took off Clarabelle's pillow in the back of the blue Dodge. That was after you suffocated her and took the pillowcase with your fingerprints on it. You left the truck at the lake and you left the satchel behind in the bed of the truck."

Izzie's eyebrows raised and leaned forward toward Jessie.

"You are so very wrong. I do know who I'm dealing with. I'm dealing with my Daddy's killer. I heard you tell mother how you killed all three, daddy, Father Sim's and Clarabelle.

"Ya're crazy to talk like this to me. I'm someone who's been caring for you all your life. I've loved ya', your sister and mother. Ya' can't prove anything."

"Clarabelle saw you. She wrote down everything she saw in a letter to me and Hannah. You had to silence her. Dear Father Sims would've told about Daddy and the man you killed long ago if he'd got to give his confession. You sure took care this didn't happen."

"I had to avenge my Pa. I had to protect your mother from my drunken brother. I had to put the priest out of his misery. We're better off. Your damn letter, if ya' have such a thing, doesn't prove a God damn thing."

"I also know what I heard you say to mother last week when you came to see her. I heard you talking in her bedroom. Are you really Hannah's father?"

"Did you hear that?" Jessie shifted in his chair. "We were just kidding around."

"Kidding around when you talked about why you killed Daddy Matt?"

"When I killed, it was for a good reason, a good reason, ya' hear. When

I was a teenager, a young man killed my paw. Father Sims saw it all. He knew. He held my Pa as he died. I had to avenge his death. Ya' think your daddy was paralyzed when he accidently fell.

No Ma'am, on one of our wild boar huntin' trips, I aimed at his head, tripped and the bullet hit his spine. Some accident that was."

Izzie gasped. Her body froze as she stared at Jessie with wide eyes. Tears gathered. Her hands flew to cover her open mouth. Then, she began to rub the nape of her neck.

Jessie's eyes were a glassy unblinking stare. He stood, shoulders back, and glared down on us. "Olivia had previously told me what happened that New Year's Eve. The only thing to do was take care of him, rightly so. I didn't know you were in that room. Unless ya' crossed me I would never do anything to hurt ya."

"Just murder my daddy, that's all," Izzie screamed as she jumped up from the sofa.

Chapter 40

"Stop screaming, you stupid girl. If ya' know so much then where's that damn letter you said was your proof? Ya're a liar like ya' dad. He never admitted to me he took advantage of Olivia. Trying to make me think ya' know so much. Where's the damn letter?"

"You think I made it all up about Clarabelle's letter. I'm lucky I found it. She had it safely hidden for years. I'll show you. Move Sammy. You're in my way. I'll get him the letter."

I knew to follow Izzie. She headed to the bow of the boat and slammed the cabin door against the wall.

"Ya' think ya' know so damn much," Jessie yelled. "Ya' shoulda' left this matter alone. Ya' and that damned dog might get hurt. I came prepared just in case ya' pulled a stunt like this."

I hopped off the sofa and followed Izzie. My sideways glance saw Jessie as he leaned down to the table and picked up the candy box. I wondered why Jessie did that. What was in the box? Jessie gazed down at his hand holding something like a little flashlight.

I was frantic and afraid as I ran to catch up with Izzie. Her hands grabbed me as I went through the door. With one step she was on the top bunk bed and pushed me out the porthole. I heard Jessie cussing as Izzie followed me through the same porthole. Before I could figure out what was happening, Izzie grabbed me, and we jumped off the boat into the water.

It might have been the dog days of summer, but that river was cold. One of us was shaking, maybe me, maybe sweet momma. Izzie told me to swim, kick my legs. A burst of energy grabbed me. I was kicking fast and furious. We began swimming toward the harbor when I heard a crack, a snap, a sound like a million firecrackers at the Dog Daze of Summer barbeque. I looked back to see the water on fire. A police siren was blasting. My young legs paddled frantically against the current. My breath was short. Momma held me by the hook on my life jacket.

Logs and debris floated around us. Sweet Momma had a tight grasp on me as she lunged for one of the logs. She missed. A wave from a passing fishing boat pushed us toward the shore. She swam. I kicked.

I looked toward the shore and saw Jake take off his shoes. He dove into the water while two men in grey uniforms, hands on hips, stood on the bank.

I panted as Jake put his arms around us and guided us toward the shoreline. I felt Izzie relax as she gasped for air and held me tighter. We all wheezed as we fell on the sand. My beautiful fur was oily and wet. What had just happened? I didn't know, but I knew I was safe. Hannah and Patrick came running toward us. Hannah took hold of me, removed my life jacket, and fiercely rubbed me with a towel.

A lick on Hannah's pale face told her I was okay. I ran to Izzie and set my bottom on her wet foot. I looked up to see Jake grasp her face.

Drops of water ran over his hands. He pushed a strand of hair from her face. A droplet of water ran over her eyebrow and down her cheek. Another droplet dripped from her nose onto her lips. Suddenly Jake kissed her.

That kiss was gentle. I know because Izzie didn't yell. Instead she quietly said, "What are you doing?"

"Izzie, I've tried to tell you so many times. Remember the letter from Mother? I've been wanting to read it to you." Jake still held her face. "The letter will explain our parent's past, it will change our lives, our future. Matt was not my real dad. You are not my half-sister. Gianni Rocco is my dad."

Izzie's arms encircled Jake's waist. Her lips parted slightly. She only smiled, said nothing.

"The secret emotion I've felt for you was not the love of a brother toward a sister but the passion a man has for the woman whose presence gave him the warmth of a kindred spirit."

"Kiss me again." Izzie leaned forward until their bodies made contact. Her arms moved up to caress Jake's shoulders. Her breathing quickened.

A red and white van appeared and people in white coats sprinted toward us. Izzie and Jake paid no attention.

Neither did I.

I wondered, where was Uncle Jessie?

I watched as Jake took Izzie's hand in his and kissed it.

Life was good. I wagged my tail. Tap. Tap. Tap.

The End

Epilogue

Explosion Rocks Memphis River Port
David King
Memphis Commercial Times
USA TODAY NETWORK – Tennessee

An explosion, yesterday, July twenty-eight, at five-forty-five, CST, rocked the Memphis River Pier off the Port of Presidents Island. The Coast Guard and Memphis Police Marine units were immediately dispatched to the scene. In the blast, a cruiser owned by Izzie and Hannah DeLisle was destroyed.

According to Memphis police, Izzie Delisle and her dog were on the boat but escaped the blast by swimming to shore. Both were treated by the Memphis Fire Depart Paramedics and released. Jessie DeLisle, who was on the boat at that time, has not been seen nor his body recovered.

Police investigators, at the time of this report, are baffled by the cause of this violent explosion. Authorities were hesitant to speculate on the blast, saying only that it was caused by some type of high-powered device. Police cordoned off a three-square block area, blocking traffic and crowds who came to look in the afternoon drizzle.

Due to the swift current of the Mississippi River, much of the evidence has been swept downstream. Residents in regions south of Memphis are asked to be to on high alert for debris and possible human remains.

Thank You

Dear Reader,

Thank you for taking the time to read Dog Daze of Summer. If you enjoyed it, please consider telling your friends and posting a short review. Word of mouth is an author's best friend, helps more than you could possibly know, and is much appreciated.

About the Author

When Maryanne VanDyke started a book club in Southern Illinois fifty years ago, she never dreamed she would write her debut novel at the age of eighty-two.

Although VanDyke was a free-lance writer for the Evansville Courier in Evansville, Indiana and, later, for the City of Phoenix employee Newsletter, she had never written fiction. In 1995 she moved to Bella Vista, Arkansas and joined the Village Writing School in Eureka Springs. Under their tutorage she quickly began a southern adult mystery novel as told from the point of view of her Shih Tzu, Sam.

Upon moving to Smyrna, Tennessee, she joined a creative writing class at the Senior Center where she continued to embrace her mantra – repotyourlife – believing change to be the initial step toward growth no matter what your age.

VanDyke lives with Sam the Shih Tzu in Smyrna, Tennessee. Writing has become her passion as she consults with her furry super sleuth for the next three novels in their Dog-Tail Detective Series. When not writing, she teaches Mah Jongg and works at her new business venture, The Tipsy Concierge. Sam is rarely far from her lap.

Reach her on Facebook: Maryanne VanDyke, Author or maryannevandykeauthor@gmail.com

Made in the USA
Lexington, KY
12 December 2019